The Brown House Stories

The Brown House Stories

A Child's Garden of Eden

NYLE KARDATZKE

Editorial Services: Karen Roberts, RQuest, LLC

Cover illustration: Dr. Glenda Ison

Photo on back cover by Rob Nichols

Printed in the United States of America

For permission to use material, contact:

Nyle Kardatzke
Email: nylebk@gmail.com

ISBN-13: 9781514688977
ISBN-10: 1514688972

Contents

Preface

These stories are all true. At least each story is based on something that really happened. They are memories from a small boy who was three years old when he lived in a house in rural Ohio known to him simply as "the Brown House." When he was three, his family moved from the Brown House, and he took his memories with him. I was that small boy.

Some of the stories are based on incidents of which I have distinct, detailed memories, such as "Stolen Fudge," "Scaring the Brown House Bear," and "Walking on the Water." Other stories have grown from only the tiniest seed of fact that I heard from my parents after I grew up and became a four-year-old or even older. These stories include "Pearl Harbor Day," "Hiding in the Smokehouse," and "Tragedy Roars By."

How to Enjoy This Book

These stories have been written for adults to read for their own enjoyment. Teachers, parents, and grandparents may choose to read some of them aloud to children. If they are read aloud to children, some stories may benefit from the historical and geographical background included near at the end the book. Also included at the end of the book are questions for conversations that may be fun to use with children, either at home or in classrooms.

The Brown House Today

Electricity and indoor plumbing had not yet reached the brown house, but planes roared overhead, cars and trucks were common, and trains called children's imaginations to faraway places. Bears existed only in folk tales and children's imaginations, but one bear seemed especially real. In the summer of 1943, the family moved away, taking with them stories of that little brown house. That move confirms the timeframe of these stories.

The Brown House is still there today, but it's not brown anymore. It now has yellow siding, so others might call it "the Yellow House." The house has sometimes been white, and once it was blue, but it has always been the Brown House to my family and me. We still love to remember when we lived there.

The boys who lived there in 1943 are now old men, and several different families have lived in the Brown House over the years. People still live in the Brown House. If they have small children, I hope those kids discover that the Brown House is a wonderful place to learn what it's like to be alive and free in the world.

Nyle, Owen, and Merl Kardatzke at the Brown House in July 1943

Acknowledgments

For the actual events in these stories I am indebted especially to my parents, Arlin and Ruth Kardatzke, who saw me safely through these adventures when they were a young married couple. My brothers, Merl and Owen, have provided factual corrections, which I have generally accepted. Owen read all of the stories in an early draft and made detailed comments. Merl remembers "Leaky Lucky" differently than I, but I'm not troubled by his actual memory of Leaky Lucky. I'm sticking with my version.

My editor, Karen Roberts, helped me work through many drafts and many corrections, and I thank her for her patience as well as her professional skill.

I am grateful for the input of several teachers and friends. Deborah Reidy and Elaine Sandy read the entire document and made detailed comments and corrections. They also made insightful additions to the Questions for Conversations at the end of the book. Deborah teaches at Sycamore School, Indianapolis; Elaine Sandy, one of the school's founders, recently retired from the school. Karen Haensch, one of my high school classmates and a retired English teacher, read a late draft of the book and made helpful, encouraging comments. I received encouragement from Eileen Prince at Sycamore School and Brian Wolf at Brookfield Academy. Two lifelong friends, Karla Telfer and Jody Donovan, read the stories and raised helpful questions.

Jeannette Hommel, age twelve, daughter of friends in Indianapolis, read the stories and drew some pen and ink sketches. You will find her artwork on the five part opener pages. I am grateful for her work to enhance the book.

The cover is a watercolor painting by Dr. Glenda Ison Bower of Topeka, Kansas. Glenda is the daughter of Lucille Ison, who for many years drew cartoons of playful elves for *Wee Wisdom Magazine.*

Needless to say, none of these accomplices is to be blamed for errors and vagaries that remain. I have had plenty of chances to make corrections, but I probably have failed here and there. I hope you find the stories entertaining, but not for any remaining blunders you may find.

Why the House Was Called Brown

The Brown House was about a mile from the small town of Graytown, in northwest Ohio. It was about ten miles south of Lake Erie and twenty miles east of Toledo. A train line that ran from Chicago to New York went through Graytown, so the family that lived in the house could hear many trains each day.

The Brown House was part of an old-fashioned farm, not like most American farms today. It was more like farms in the 1800s than farms today. Cows, chickens, pigs, and horses lived in the barns. A farmer worked the land and used the barns. My family rented the Brown House, and the farmer managed the rest of the farm.

The Brown House was surrounded by trees that gave shade in the summer, and one tree stretched out a limb that held up a swing. Behind the house was a large yard with a sandbox. Farm fields surrounded the house on three sides. On the fourth side, in front of the house, stood a barn and other farm buildings. Between the house and the barn was a large, gravel-covered area that city people might call a parking lot.

Country people called it a barnyard. Huge wagons of hay or grain from the fields used the barnyard for turning around and unloading.

The Brown House got its name because it was brown. It was covered on the roof and sides with brown wooden shingles that made it look warm and friendly. The house was small, with an upstairs and a downstairs, no electricity, no running water, and no indoor toilet. Light came from kerosene lamps. Water came from a hand pump in the kitchen that drew water from a shallow well just outside the house. Pushing down on the pump handle a few times brought cold water to the sink any time of year. The family toilet was an outhouse, a small building that sat above a deep hole in the backyard. The Brown House was typical of the way most people lived in the 1940s, and it was a good way to live.

My family lived in the Brown House for two years, from May 1941 until July 1943. At that time, my family consisted of Mama and Daddy, my older brother Merl, my younger brother Owen, and me. World War II started while we lived there, but we were far from the war, and it seemed not to affect our lives.

I was born in a rented farmhouse on the outskirts of the village of Lindsey, Ohio, in 1939, but I remember nothing from that house. My mind and memory were awakened at the Brown House. It was my Garden of Eden. It was a beautiful, quiet place for small boys to live. In that quiet place there were adventures, surprises, and some scary times. This book tells the best stories that happened while my family and I lived in the Brown House.

Part One

DISCOVERING THE WORLD

One

Seeing the World from the Windmill

An old-fashioned windmill towered over the driveway at the Brown House, and the metal fan at the top looked like a very large pinwheel. A long metal rod connected the fan to a pump at the bottom. When the wind picked up enough to move the blades of the fan, the rod went up and down to pump water from the well under the windmill. Windmills like this were on all the farms in those days because most farms didn't have electricity, and it was too much work to stand and pump all day to get enough water for the horses and cows to drink. With a windmill, the wind did the work.

Our windmill was not like the enormous windmills you now see on "wind farms," with their huge propellers. Those modern windmills are much taller, and they generate electricity from the wind. The old windmills did work directly, rather than generating electricity to do the work.

To me the most important thing about the windmill was the ladder to the top. It was a row of metal steps on one of the windmill's four legs. The steps were also the handles for climbing. The steps were not made for a young boy like me, but if I pulled a little wagon over and stood on it on my tiptoes, I could climb up onto the first step. Then I could reach each step and go higher and higher. The cold feel of the metal steps was exciting and made me want to climb to the very top. The windmill must have been only twenty feet tall, but it was high enough to give me a good look at the world around me.

My brothers and I played outside a lot while Daddy was at work and Mama was working in the house. We loved the freedom of playing outside without our parents to watch over us, and we thought all kids played like that and always would.

One summer day I made my way to the base of the windmill and looked up at the top. White, fluffy clouds hung high in the sky above the windmill. There wasn't enough wind to turn the windmill's fan blades that day, but the clouds and sky seemed to call me to climb the ladder. "Nyle!" they called to me. "Come up and see the world!"

I wasn't supposed to climb the windmill, but I didn't know it yet. No one had told me because I was so little, but I soon learned. That day I had climbed up only a few steps of the ladder when suddenly someone grabbed my feet. It was the babysitter! If I had been just a little faster, she couldn't have reached me.

"Come back down here!" she yelled. "You'll fall down from there!"

She kept pulling at my feet until I had to let go. She caught me and put me on the ground. "You're not supposed to climb the windmill!" she said. "Now go and play somewhere else."

I went away to the sandbox, but I looked back at the windmill. It must be a very special thing if the babysitter didn't want me to climb it, I thought. It must be very fun and important. The sandbox in the backyard now wasn't as much fun as it had been. I decided I would wait for a time when the babysitter wasn't watching and try to climb the windmill again.

My chance came on a day when the babysitter was gone. Mama was at home, but she was taking an afternoon nap. The clouds were there again, and they seemed to be calling, "Now is the time! Come on up! Climb the windmill!"

I looked around to make sure no one was looking. I began to climb. I pulled myself up onto the first step. Already I could look down at the driveway and between two of the sheds near the barn. I stretched for another handhold and pulled myself higher. I was about halfway to the top of the windmill when something bad happened.

"Hey! Nyle's climbing the windmill!" my older brother, Merl, yelled. "He's way up high!"

I knew I had to hurry to reach the top. I pulled up another step, and I was so high that not even a grown-up could grab my feet.

"Come back down!" Merl yelled. "I'm going to tell Mama!"

I didn't say anything and made it onto another step. Just then Mama came out of the house.

"Nyle! What are you doing? Come back down here!" she called.

I knew my climb was over, so I took a quick look around. There were fields on the other side of the corncrib, and I could see the young soybeans growing there. Farther away I could see the big trees and some of the houses in Graytown, where the train tracks were. I looked as far as I could all around, and I could tell that it was a big world, bigger than the Brown House and even bigger than the barn.

"He doesn't know how to get down," Mama said. "Can you help him, Merl?"

"Sure," Merl said, and he started climbing the ladder toward me.

"I can do it!" I yelled. "I'm coming down. Let me do it!"

I started down, and Merl went down too. He waited at the bottom of the ladder. When I reached the extra-long step at the bottom of the ladder, I stopped.

"Help him down, Merl," Mama said.

Merl wrapped his arms around me and set me on the ground. I had felt big and important on my climb, but I felt like a little kid when he put me down. I felt like a three-year-old.

It was good to be back on the ground, but it was also good to remember the thrill of being up high. I couldn't wait to be bigger and climb clear to the top of the windmill. Then I would stay a long time and see as much of the world as possible. What would I see from up there? Would I be able to see an ocean or a mountain from up there? Could I see a foreign country? Would I ever go to the places I could see?

The windmill taught me to climb up and look far, far away and to imagine places like Africa and Asia and Indiana and Oklahoma. I would be a traveler someday, I thought, and go to all of the places I could see and imagine.

After many years, I did go to mountains, oceans, lakes, deserts, and seas. I also went to foreign countries. I saw big cities and small villages. I couldn't see those places from the windmill in Ohio. I couldn't even see Lake Erie from there, but I started to think about faraway places that day. I hope kids can still climb trees and go high in buildings, even if they can't see the whole world from a windmill.

For more about windmills, see "Background Information" at the back of this book.

Two

The Beacon Light

One night my older brother and I slept in the other upstairs bedroom, the spare one in the back of the house. After Mama tucked us in, she went downstairs and took the kerosene lamp with her. The room was dark, but a bright white light suddenly flashed in through the window. It raced across the room and disappeared. Soon a blue light flashed across and then another white light.

"What is it?" I asked Merl.

"It's just the beacon light. Don't be scared."

"Does it always shine like that? What's it doing?"

Merl knew about a lot of things, since he was already six years old and had started school. He told me about beacon lights and why airplanes needed them. He was still talking when I fell asleep.

Beacon lights were similar to lighthouses along the shores of oceans and lakes. Beacon lights were placed on land to help airplane pilots find their way through the great ocean of air, much like lighthouses helped ships find their way. Beacon lights even looked like lighthouses. Their light sat high on a tower where it could be seen for many miles around, like the light on a lighthouse. The beacon light I saw shining through the window that night stood on a farm only a mile from the Brown House, on Elliston Road.

A man or sometimes a family lived next to the beacon light to make sure it was on at all times, just like lighthouses had lighthouse keepers. All night long, the beacon light went round and round to help show airplane pilots the way to go in the dark.

Many airplanes flew over the Brown House, and they needed that beacon light. A few were passenger planes, and some carried important mail, back then known as Air Mail. Some were warplanes, because we lived in the Brown House during World War II. The closest airport was in the city of Toledo, less than twenty miles away. I thought it was a big, important airport, but that's because Toledo had the only airport I knew about.

In those days no one in our family ever rode in an airplane. We had no reason to ride in one. We only heard them going overhead and sometimes saw them on clear days. During the day when we heard one, we would look up to try to see it. At night, after my brothers and I were in bed, we listened for them and watched the beacon light's path.

All of the airplanes in those days had propellers. Jet airplanes had not yet been invented. Airplanes with propellers were very noisy, and they flew much lower than today's jets do. We could hear those propeller airplanes coming, hear them fly over, and hear them going off into the distance. They were so loud we could feel the noise in our chests. They flew so low we could see them easily in daytime if the sky was clear. At night we could just see the lights at the tips of their wings.

The airplanes that flew over the Brown House did not have all of the instruments that planes have today. Some of them had radios for talking to airports and to other planes, but most didn't have instruments to show the pilots where they were. In daytime, the pilots could find where they were from paper maps, a compass, and also towns, roads, and rivers they could see on the ground. At night, pilots had to look for beacon lights.

As I got older, I learned that at night, almost everything on the ground looks black from an airplane. A pilot couldn't find his airport at night by looking at roads and rivers because he couldn't see them. Beacon lights helped the pilot by showing him the way.

Beacon lights must have been especially welcome to pilots in foggy weather or when a storm was coming in. They must have been a comfort, too, for passengers who were scared up there in the black sky, looking down at the black earth, seeing only a few pinpoints of light. When the beacon light near the Brown House appeared far off on the horizon, the pilot and his navigator on the plane would check their maps and compass. Any fear they might have had about their location would leave them. Their hearts would beat a little slower, knowing just where their plane was in that vast, black night. Before long, the lights of the airport would come into view to help them make a safe landing.

When the beacon light shone on the walls of the Brown House, it made us feel safe. It also made people safe as they flew over through the night sky. We felt sure that when we were big enough to travel in an airplane, there would be beacon lights to help our plane find where it was going and lead us back home again.

You probably know that beacon lights are rare now. You may see them at airports, but not on farms like the one I knew about in Ohio. Beacon lights are not necessary anymore because airplanes now have wonderful instruments that show the pilots exactly where their planes are. These are better times for travel, but kids no longer have the fun of watching beacon lights shine into their rooms at night.

For additional information about early aviation beacon lights, see "Background Information" at the end of this book.

Three

TRAIN WHISTLE BLOWING

Graytown is a small railroad town about a mile up the road from the Brown House. Hundreds of these railroad towns existed across the United States. They were built when trains were the main way to go to faraway places. Railroad towns had passenger stations called depots, and they had freight loading docks where big boxes of toys and cookies and other important things were loaded. Some railroad towns grew into good size cities, but most railroad towns like Graytown stayed very small. Some disappeared completely when people moved away from the country and into the cities. Graytown remained small, and it's still there today.

Trains at that time were the kind with big, black engines that huffed and puffed and blew out towers of black smoke. Those trains operated on steam from boiling water, and they burned coal to heat the water. Everything near the train track got dirty with the soot from those trains. (Maybe that's how Graytown got its name, but Blacktown might have been a better name.)

Railroad towns had piles of coal to burn in the train engines and water towers so the trains could fill up with water to make the steam that moved their great steel wheels. Some also had tall buildings called "elevators" that held grain until it was loaded onto trains. Wheat, oats, corn, and soybeans were loaded from the elevators into the train cars and then hauled to cities to be made into bread, oatmeal, cereal, and cookies.

You couldn't ride in a grain elevator. They were called elevators because grain was lifted into bins very high up so it could flow down into train cars by gravity. You can still see lots of grain elevators in farm country.

A very important train line ran between Chicago and New York City, and it went right through Graytown. My favorite trains were the passenger trains that carried only people. They were the fastest and made the ground shake the most. I liked to imagine riding on them. Some of the passengers went all the way from New York City to California, from the Atlantic Ocean to the Pacific Ocean.

Almost every small town had a passenger train station in those days, so people could go almost anywhere on a train. Most passenger trains didn't stop at Graytown. They just went thundering through. But two passenger trains did stop in Graytown every day.

Once or twice my family had to stop in our car and wait for a passenger train to go by at night. For a few moments, I could see people in the lighted cars reading, eating, talking, and sleeping. They sped past us in their own special world that was taking them between the worlds where they lived and where they were going. The people on the trains seemed like kings and queens and presidents, so different from all of us.

When trains went through Graytown, the air was torn by the noise of their whistles. Train whistles back then were loud and scary. They seemed to me like the end of the world was coming. Their whistles made several notes at the same time, unlike the smooth, single tone of modern diesel engines.

On a very quiet night, I could hear a train as it crossed farm roads when it was two miles away. The sound would become louder and louder until the train reached Graytown. Then it would shake the ground, and its whistle would howl like an angry animal. I could listen to its great, powerful sound until it went off into the distance. The quiet sound of the train coming seemed like something important about to happen. The loud noise when it was near was like the middle of something big and great, or maybe like the middle of an exciting story. As the train went away, it sounded like something ending, going away to where memories are kept.

Not many years after we moved from the Brown House, the steam trains stopped coming, and we never heard their huge whistles again. We didn't see their clouds of heavy black smoke, either. Steam trains were replaced by the kind you see today, which are pulled by diesel oil-burning engines. It used to take as many as five or six men to drive the old steam trains, but two or three men can drive the new ones. Coal-burning steam engines used more fuel than the new diesels, too, so they were more expensive to operate. And those steam-powered train engines could pull only short trains compared to what today's train engines can pull.

When the use of steam-powered engines stopped, some people were happy. The new trains didn't drop black soot over the towns along their way. The bad thing about the new trains was that they didn't have really loud whistles, only horns that sounded like car horns. It was as though a trombone or the voice of a choir singer had replaced the voice of a big, strong workman on a steam train.

Some people liked the new horns, but most of us who heard the steam whistles blowing on the New York Central line in the 1940s will always think of those as the *real* trains with *real* whistles and *real* smoke, calling people to ride away on them or at least to dream about riding away to all the places where trains go.

For additional information about early Ohio railroads, see "Background Information" at the end of this book.

Four

GRAYTOWN PARK

It was almost always quiet at the Brown House except when planes flew over or when trains went through Graytown. Most of the time my brothers and I were happy to play in the house or in the yard, but sometimes it was fun to go some other place to play. One of our favorite places to go to was Graytown Park.

For such a small town, Graytown had a fine park. It was a large, square, flat parcel of land with a farm field on two sides. It had a large shelter house and a play area for kids. Families could have reunions and church groups could have Sunday school picnics in the shelter house. We kids had no interest in the shelter house because to us it was just a big, boring place for grown-ups. What we liked were the rides in the play area.

Most of the rides we liked best at Graytown Park were there until I was a grown man, and I took my children there whenever we visited Ohio. Most of those old rides are now considered too dangerous, and you won't find them in parks anywhere, not even at Graytown. I'll tell you about them so you'll know what you missed.

First, there were the metal slides. These slides had steep metal ladders that we had to climb carefully, holding on to metal handrails. When we reached the top, we would sit, look down briefly to see where we were going, and then slide straight down on the slick, sloping metal between the smooth metal sides. If we were lucky, we would go so fast we would fall down when we reached the bottom.

At Graytown Park there were two slides, a big one and a small one. Both slides were fun in good weather, but they could be freezing cold in cooler weather. Sometimes in the summer when the sun was out, they could be too hot to touch. After a rain, the slides were wet and extra slippery, and often there was a big puddle at the bottom to land in or try to jump over.

The big slide had a hump in the middle. We would slide down quickly about half way, slow down a little in the flatter section in the middle, and then drop fast to the bottom of the slide after the hump. The wind would blast our faces as we slid, and we'd have a funny feeling in our stomachs when we went over the hump. That slide was our favorite, so we rode it over and over until our legs were tired from climbing the ladder or until somebody got hurt.

One time a really bad thing happened on the slides. Some bigger kids from town came to the park while my brothers and I were there with Mama. One of the big kids climbed to the top of the big slide and just sat at the top. When we climbed the ladder to ride, he did a nasty thing. He turned around and spat on us! We climbed back down and told Mama. She told the boy to stop spitting and get down. He wouldn't obey, so we went home. We didn't want to play with kids who did such nasty things.

Besides the slides, there were teeter-totters. You may have seen or even played on teeter-totters at some older parks, but they are nearly extinct now. A teeter-totter was mainly a board balanced over a pipe about two feet off the ground. Two people could ride on a teeter-totter, with one at each end of the board. Sometimes two kids could be at each end if the teeter-totter had a long enough board.

Kids on a teeter-totter took turns riding slowly up and down, with each person pushing gently off when his feet hit the ground so he would go up and the other person would go down. On a big teeter-totter, the person at the high point of the ride would be higher than the head of a grownup.

There were four teeter-totters at Graytown Park, all alike. None of them had handles for the riders, so we just had to "hold on for dear life," as we said in those days. We were supposed to ride up and down slowly and gently, but sometimes we pushed off from the ground so hard that the person on the other end nearly flew off. When someone pushed off really hard on purpose, the board would drop out from under the kid at the high end as he went down. For half a second, that kid was almost weightless, like in a spaceship.

It was against the rules to jump off the teeter-totter when someone was high in the air on the other side. When someone broke that rule, the other person would drop to the ground suddenly and have a hurt bottom. I remember kids getting into big trouble for making little kids drop too fast. I was one of the little kids, and I thought the teeter-totters were scary to ride unless Mama was there to watch over me.

Best of all were the merry-go-rounds. Three merry-go-rounds were at Graytown Park. The safest one looked like a large metal birdcage, and the littlest kids liked that one. A tall metal pipe stood straight up in the middle. At the top was a metal wheel on its side. Thinner pipes came out from the center of the wheel like spokes on a bicycle wheel. Those pipes bent down, and wooden benches were attached on each one, making seats for kids to ride. The wooden benches were about knee high from the ground, so little kids could easily hop on.

To make the merry-go-round work, some kids could sit on the benches while other kids grabbed hold and ran alongside to make the whole merry-go-round spin. We probably could have loaded twenty or thirty kids onto that merry-go-round, but we never had more than three or four kids at any one time at Graytown Park. To make it move with just a few kids, we would sit on the benches and push with one foot on the ground while we were riding. Sometimes one or two kids would run and push before jumping on. It was a fun, safe ride. For me it was too safe to be really, really fun.

Another of the merry-go-rounds had a round metal platform just a few inches off the ground. The riders stood or sat at the edges of the metal platform and grasped the pipes attached to it for handles with their feet dangling off the edge of the platform. Some kids would run around the outside to push the merry-go-round and get it going. They would then try to jump on. When the merry-go-round was going really fast, the riders could feel themselves being pulled to the edge, and sometimes they even went flying off.

We kids learned that something called centrifugal force was pulling us to the edge, but we didn't know the word *centrifugal*. We also learned it was safer if we didn't get the merry-go-round going too fast. If we did, we might fly off at high speed, hit the ground, or get our feet twisted and hurt under the spinning platform. This merry-go-round was fun for me, especially when I got dizzy, jumped off, and fell down on the ground.

The third merry-go-round was the favorite, the fastest, and the most dangerous one by far. It was also the smallest. It was made for only two riders. The riders sat on wooden seats facing each other at opposite ends of a metal bar that was attached to an axle in the middle of the ride. Each rider had a hand bar to pull toward him with his hands and a bar to push forward with his feet. A crank in the middle of the ride was attached to the riders' push and pull bars.

To make the ride move, one rider would pull the hand bar back as he pushed his feet forward, and the other rider did the opposite. The action made the merry-go-round spin faster and faster. To make this merry-go-round spin at top speed, the two riders had to take turns pushing and pulling, leaning far back as they pulled and pushed.

When my brothers were older, we could work up tremendous speed on this two-person merry-go-round. The only thing that kept us from falling off was holding onto the hand bar "for dear life." If we let go for even a second, we would go flying off into the grass.

When we rode this one, we liked to make it spin as fast as possible for as long as possible, until all we could see of the world around us was a blur of lines. When we got off, we were so dizzy we would fall down. Some kids even threw up. Even so, it was a lot of fun. If a kid didn't know about centrifugal force before he went on this ride, he knew about it when he got off, especially if he flew off into the grass.

We kids kept going to Graytown Park after we moved from the Brown House in 1943. As we got bigger, we could do even more dangerous things on the slides and go faster than ever on the merry-go-rounds. Even now, as old man, I think about riding one of the merry-go-rounds until I was so dizzy I would fall down when I got off. Maybe there will be one of those merry-go-rounds in heaven.

Playgrounds for kids these days are better than Graytown Park in some ways. The new ones are safer, and they have more things to do. But if kids or their families see a park with old-fashioned rides like we had in Graytown, I hope they remember this story and take a few rides. And I hope they ride responsibly and safely.

Five

Our Own Merry-Go-Round

We kids had our own merry-go-round at the Brown House. It was not the kind at a town park, an amusement park, or a circus. It wasn't even the kind we played on at Graytown Park. Daddy made our merry-go-round. To us, it was one of the "funnest" things in the yard.

Our merry-go-round spun around a tall post about five feet tall that was stuck deep in the ground. The post was like an extra-large wooden fence post. On top of it was a wheel that turned, and on top of the wheel was a long board. A swing hung down from each end of the board. The seats at the bottom of the ropes were about a foot from the ground.

When kids sat in the swing seats, they could take a ride on the merry-go-round if a big person pushed the board and made it go around. If no one was there to push, each kid could kick off with his feet to get the swings moving. That made for a slow ride. The best rides were when a bigger kid or a grown-up pushed us.

A really strong pusher who wanted to give us a really good ride would tell us to get on our seats and hold on tight. He would then put his hands onto the side of the board and run in a circle, faster and faster. As the board went faster, the swing seats would rise up until they were nearly straight out. When the pusher couldn't run any faster or got tired, he would duck his head and run out of the way. For a while, the merry-go-round would keep going around until it finally slowed down and stopped.

We kids took turns at riding, and any kids who were tall enough to reach the board could be pushers. A really good ride was when we went so fast that when we got off, we were dizzy and fell down, just like when we rode the bigger merry-go-rounds at Graytown Park. Somehow falling down was an important sign to us that we were having fun.

Because we kids loved it so much and because he had done such a good job of building it, Daddy took our merry-go-round apart and moved it to our new house when we left the Brown House. For a long time I didn't know there were kids who didn't have their own merry-go-rounds at home. I thought all kids had them.

Several years later, at the new house, Daddy built us an even better merry-go-round. It went faster than any other merry-go-round we knew. He built this one with an old truck axle that he bought at a junkyard. He took off one of the wheels and put that end of the axle in a deep hole in the ground so the axle stood straight up in the air and the other wheel was on top. He poured a lot of cement in the hole and made sure the axle stayed straight up until the cement dried into concrete.

Daddy then bolted a very thick, wide, and long board across the top of the wheel. That board was called a "two by ten." It was about two inches thick and ten inches wide – a very strong board. After the board was on, Daddy put a swing with ropes and a wooden seat at each end of the board, just like we had on our old merry-go-round. Finally, he put a steering wheel on the side of the axle to use as a crank. The steering wheel was connected to the drive shaft that once had connected the truck's engine to its back wheels to make them turn around. The person giving rides on this merry-go-round took the place of the engine that had made the truck go.

To make this merry-go-round work, two kids would get into the swings, and a big kid or a grown-up would get in the middle and turn the steering wheel. The person turning the wheel had to duck his head to be under the board as it spun around faster and faster and faster. At top speed, the kids in the swing seats would be flying straight out. It was never good to get in the way of the flying riders, and it was especially bad to fall off those swings.

We were so lucky that Daddy liked to build fun rides for kids at the Brown House and at our new house. Unlike at amusement parks, we never had to pay to ride on our merry-go-rounds. We only had to pay by taking turns pushing. We had plenty of time and plenty of energy, and we had very little money. We were happy to pay for our rides by giving rides.

My father's inventiveness is reported further in "Background Information" at the end of this book.

Six

Fire Made from Dirt

When I got up from my afternoon nap one day at the Brown House, I went outside and smelled a really nice smell. A thin line of fire was burning slowly in the dry grass among the trees in the orchard. The smoke from the burning grass was what smelled so good. To me it smelled even better than the smell of leaves burning in the fall.

I walked a little closer and saw Daddy working around the fire. I liked to see fire, so I watched what Daddy was doing. He was raking up some dry grass. "Hi there!" he yelled to me. "Don't get too close to the fire! Stay over there and watch."

Soon some of the fire started coming toward where I was standing in the lawn. Daddy picked up a shovel and came to me. Using his shovel, he dug into the lawn near the fire, and it looked to me as though his digging was starting new fires. Then he went back to rake more grass in the orchard.

I had a small shovel, so I decided to try to start a fire by digging the way Daddy did. I took my shovel to the place where Daddy had dug in the lawn and turned over some of the dry soil. Nothing happened. I tried a few more times, but no fire. That night at supper, I didn't ask Daddy how he did it. I was pretty sure he wouldn't want me to start a fire.

A couple of days later, I took my shovel and went to the same place in the yard where it seemed Daddy had made fire by digging. I looked around to be sure no one saw me. Then I started digging again, trying to do it exactly the way Daddy had done. Once again, nothing happened. There wasn't even any good smelling smoke, only dust from the dirt.

I kept digging a while longer, hoping to start a fire, but no fire started, so I gave up. Daddy must have had a special way of digging dirt to cause a fire, I thought. I tried once or twice again on other days, but no fire started.

I learned much later that Daddy was *stopping* the fire with dirt, not *starting* fire. He was digging into the lawn to create a line of dirt to stop the grass fire from coming too far into the lawn. By the time I learned this, I was probably about six years old. By then I knew more, and I could see how much smarter I was than when I was only a little kid.

If you live in the city, you may not have had a chance to smell burning grass or leaves. People aren't allowed to burn things in most cities now. That's one of the bad things about living in the city. In the country, farmers still burn grass in certain fields to make way for new grass. If you are lucky, you may see a farmer burning grass and have a chance to smell it. If you get that chance, take a good whiff, but don't get too close!

Part Two

ADVENTURING AT HOME

Seven

GOING SWIMMING

One very hot day, Mama said, "How would you boys like to go swimming?"

Merl and I jumped up and down and slapped ourselves on the legs, yelling and squealing. Owen didn't understand, but he yelled and squealed and jumped up and down anyway.

"I pumped some water this morning," Mama announced as she led us out to the yard. "By now it should be warm enough for swimming."

At the Brown House we didn't have a pond, a lake, a river, or a swimming pool, but we still went swimming. It wasn't real swimming, but we didn't know what real swimming was. What we called swimming was sitting in a big wooden tub of water out in the yard right next to the windmill. The tub was made from half of a wooden barrel that probably had been used for horses and cows to drink from. We liked getting into that big wooden tub, and we called it swimming because of the water and because it made us feel cool on hot days.

Going Swimming

We didn't have swimming suits either, only the shorts that we wore every day in the summer. We didn't even know there was such a thing as a swimming suit. And we didn't have to take our shoes off to go swimming because we weren't wearing shoes. We went barefoot all summer except for Sunday and other days when we went to church.

Before it became our swimming pool, that old barrel probably had been used for storing sweet apple cider or for making pickles. But we didn't think about such things. It didn't smell like cider or pickles, and we wouldn't have cared if it had. We only wanted to go swimming.

Merl was so big that he could climb over the edge and get in by himself. Mama had to lift Owen and me into the swimming barrel. When all three of us boys sat down in the barrel, the water came up to our chests. We were wedged in so tightly we could hardly move our arms and legs. There's an old picture of the three of us in the barrel, smiling away because we thought we were swimming. It felt good to have the hot sun on our heads and shoulders while we sat in the cool water.

That day we weren't watching Mama carefully enough, and she decided to tease us. She went to the windmill and quietly began pumping cold water from the well below. We were so busy swimming that we didn't notice until fresh, icy water fell on us from the well pipe above.

We yelled and tried to splash the water away, and Mama laughed and laughed. She stopped the cold water, and we sat in the big barrel, thinking again that we were swimming. Then we climbed out of the barrel and ran around in the grass, yelling and warming up in the sun. After we were warm enough, we climbed back in the barrel to swim again, got back out to get warm, and continued getting warm and cool over and over. That was real swimming to us, and we loved it.

When our family moved away from the Brown House to a new place, it had a pond. We boys learned to swim in that pond and eventually in Lake Erie. In those big waters, we learned we could move our arms and legs when swimming, something we couldn't do when we were swimming in the barrel at the Brown House. We also learned that in real swimming, we could even duck our heads under water.

Swimming was so much more fun when we could run and jump in and paddle with our arms and feet. We laughed whenever we remembered how we used to go swimming in that big old barrel, but it was fun, and that's where we learned to love swimming.

Eight

Hiding in the Smokehouse

I can tell this story now and not worry about kids these days getting locked in a dark, smelly smokehouse. You may never have seen a smokehouse, and chances are you never will, but they used to be common in rural areas. In order to understand what happened that day at the Brown House, you need to know what a smokehouse was.

A smokehouse was a small building located next to a farmhouse. Most smokehouses were only about the size of a large closet. Ours was made of brick, and there was a low door just big enough that adults could walk in by bending over. Young kids could walk in by only ducking their heads. It always had a strong smell of smoke and meat because it was used for smoking hams and bacon.

When hogs were butchered on farms, the hams and bacon portions were placed in the smokehouse to be cured. They were hung from the ceiling, and a small fire of hickory wood was started on the floor. The door was then closed, and just enough air was allowed in to keep the fire smoldering, filling the little building with smoke. When they were finished, the hams and bacon were ready to be cooked and sliced. They tasted wonderful because of the smoke.

A batch of hams had to hang in the smokehouse for several weeks and then be moved to a cool place to age. This process was called curing. After they were cured, hams could be kept for a long time without a refrigerator. Most people did not have refrigerators when smokehouses were used, so they stored meat in a cold place or something called an icebox. An icebox was a large wooden container with a huge block of ice inside that kept food cold for a few days. When the block of ice melted, a new one was needed.

One day my older cousin Elaine and some other kids came to play with my brothers and me at the Brown House. After playing a while in the sandbox and getting a drink from the well pump, we decided to play hide-and-seek. It wasn't a real game of hide-and-seek, with someone being "it" and counting off while the others hid. In our game, someone just yelled, "Let's hide!" and we all ran for cover. No one was left for the "seek" part of the hide and seek.

I ran around the back of the house, looking for a good place to hide. A big, black spider was in the bush where I wanted to hide. I went to a different bush near the edge of the field, but another kid was already there. I kept running around the house until I came to the smokehouse. As I pulled on the door, my cousin Elaine ran up to warn me, "Be careful! Be sure there's no smoke!"

Elaine and I pulled the door open a crack and looked in. It was one of the darkest places I had ever seen. There were no windows, and it was black inside from years of smoking hams. The smell inside was strong, but it wasn't a bad smell.

"Hurry, get in!" Elaine said. She and I both went in and shut the door, leaving it open a crack to give us air and light. Soon it was very, very quiet. No one came looking for us, because everyone was hiding and nobody was "it."

Finally we heard two other kids talking in the yard. They were tired of hiding and wanted to do something else. We could hear them coming toward us, and one of them said, "That? Oh, that's the smokehouse."

We listened as they came closer. When we knew they were about to open the door, Elaine flung it open wide and let out a blood-curdling scream. The two kids screamed and turned to run, but one of them ran into the other and they both fell down. They started to cry, and Elaine laughed. I didn't know whether to laugh or cry, since I wasn't scared and I hadn't scared anybody.

All of a sudden Mama came running from the house. "What's going on? Who's hurt?" she demanded.

"Nobody's hurt," Elaine said. "They just fell down when we came out of the smokehouse."

"She scared us!" the kids whimpered, but Mama ignored them.

"What were you doing in the smokehouse?" Mama asked.

Elaine looked at me, and I looked at Mama. "We were just hiding," I said.

"Well, don't hide in there anymore," she said. "It's nasty in there."

We didn't say anything, but I thought about the smokehouse. It seemed better than ever because Mama had said it was *nasty*! I had never been in a nasty place before, and I was proud to have been in one. The other kids looked at each other and then at Elaine and me. I could tell they were jealous.

I never again hid in a smokehouse. After my family moved to a new house that didn't have a smokehouse, all I could do was remember that creepy, dark, smoky, nasty place where I hid just once. I found other places to hide at the new house, but none were as smelly, mysterious, or nasty as the smokehouse.

Nine

WALKING ON THE WATER

We went to church a lot when we lived at the Brown House. I even received a special diploma for perfect attendance at Sunday school. I still have that diploma, and I put it in a guest room at my house for visitors to see up close. It may seem like bragging until visitors actually read the diploma and see that I had perfect attendance up to five years old. The truth is, I had perfect attendance when I was very little simply because Mama and Daddy took us kids to church. If the diploma is bragging about anybody, it's about Mama and Daddy, not me.

The church my family went to was very small. The building had only one room. Before it became our church, it had been a one-room schoolhouse. About forty or fifty people came to church each Sunday, and everyone could fit in that one room. If a hundred people had come, they probably all couldn't have sat down.

Most churches had Sunday school. At our church, it was the hour before the main church service, and there were classes for all ages, even in our tiny building. For Sunday school time, the teachers hung sheets on wires like clotheslines across the room to divide it into sections. We couldn't see the other classes, but we could hear them. Everybody had to speak softly so everyone could learn Bible stories without being distracted by what was going on in the other sections.

I remember hearing lots of great Bible stories in Sunday school. Some were about the creation of the world. One was about a brave boy fighting a giant. Two stories were about Jesus feeding thousands of people and being especially nice to kids.

One of my favorite stories was about Jesus walking on the water when his friends were out in a boat in a large lake. A big storm had come up, and waves were about to tip over the boat and sink it. The friends of Jesus were really scared, but Jesus just walked on the water out to them and made the storm stop.

One of the men, a man named Peter, wanted to walk on the water, too, so Jesus told him to step out of the boat and walk to him. Peter started walking on the water, but then he got scared and stopped looking at Jesus. When he looked back at the boat, Peter began to sink into the water. Jesus had to walk over and rescue him.

I loved that story and wondered what it would be like to walk on water. At the Brown House, we didn't have a lake or a sea or even a pond. All around us were farm fields. Before the fields could be planted in the spring, the farmer who tended them had to plow the land. He pulled a great big plow behind a noisy tractor, and the plow turned over the dirt in large, curving slices that lay on top of each other like the waves of water on a lake or an ocean. To me the plowed land looked like the sea Jesus walked on when he came out to his friends in the boat, stopped the storm, and rescued them.

After the tractor and the plow were gone in the spring, my brothers and I would wait for a windy day. Then we would play "Jesus Walking on the Water." Two boys would go out into the field and pretend to be in the boat in the storm. The third boy would pretend to be Jesus. He would hold his arms out at his sides the way we thought Jesus must have done, and he would walk out to the boat. When that boy got to the boat, he would raise his arms higher to stop the storm. Then the two in the boat would clap their hands, probably because they didn't know what else to do.

Whenever we played that game, we would take turns being Jesus and being his friends in the boat until everyone had walked on the water and everyone had calmed the storm. Then we all would walk together on the water, through the plowed field, and back to our yard. I always looked back at the tossing waves in the field and thought about how much worse it would have been if those had been real waves and if the field had been a real sea. I was glad we could stand on the safe, green grass and let Jesus walk on the water.

The story of Jesus walking on the water appears in three of the four Gospels. References are listed in "Background Information" at the end of this book.

Ten

PEARL HARBOR DAY

Pearl Harbor is a beautiful bay in an island far out in the Pacific Ocean, the world's largest ocean. The United States of America has kept warships at Pearl Harbor for more than a hundred years. That island was the site of a terrible tragedy that happened during World War II while I was living at the Brown House.

In the early morning hours of Sunday, December 7, 1941, Japanese warplanes bombed Pearl Harbor in a surprise attack, destroying many American ships and airplanes and killing many people. That bombing made the United States decide to enter the war that had already started in other places of the world.

I had just turned two years old in October 1941, so I was too young to know there was a war. I learned about it later. I don't remember Pearl Harbor Day, but I remember Mama telling me about it a few years later. Those are clear memories for me still, just as you may remember hearing about something that happened before you were born.

We had no telephone, and we didn't even have a radio because we didn't have electricity for a radio. The man who owned the Brown House, George Bass, came by the day after the attack while Mama was hanging clothes outside to dry. He told Mama the bad news. She knew it meant war, and she knew that in war many bad things could happen. She cried when she heard the news because of the people who had died already and those that would die soon. Mama was only twenty-seven years old then, and she was afraid that many relatives and friends her age might have to be in the war.

After she learned the news, Mama went back to her housework. Whenever bad things happened or somebody died, she always wanted to work. It was her way of getting past the bad times and on to something better.

Pearl Harbor Day changed the lives of millions of people all over the world. It changed life for us at the Brown House too. Some people were sent overseas to be in the war, and others were given jobs back in the United Sates that would help the war effort. Daddy was already working in the Sun Oil refinery in Toledo, making gasoline for the war. Because his job was vital to the war, he didn't have to leave home to be in the war. Mama worked at Sun Oil refinery for about a year too. Her income helped pay for the house we would move into after leaving the Brown House.

Mama and Daddy didn't want us boys to know much about the war. I don't remember hearing them talk about the war while we lived at the Brown House or even at the new house. Even when Uncle Roz, Uncle Jim, and Uncle Paul came home from the war for visits to the Brown House, Mama and Daddy never talked about the war in front of us kids.

Uncle "Roz" was short for Roswell, my uncle's real name. His full name was Roswell Stagner, and he was married to my Aunt Elsie. My parents called him "Good Old Roz" because he always seemed so jolly and friendly. Uncle Roz was in the Seabees, the nickname for the Navy Construction Battalion that built airfields and hangars for airplanes after islands in the Pacific Ocean were captured. Hangars were like large garages where airplanes were repaired and spare parts were stored.

Uncle Jim Stackhouse, who was married to my Aunt Verda, was in the Navy. He was stationed on a large ship. Uncle Paul Gottke, who was married to my Aunt Marian, was a bomber pilot in the Pacific Ocean. He flew fifty-seven missions, and his plane was shot more than once. All of my uncles survived the war, and all of them and my aunts who had married them have passed away.

A lot of kids used to play imaginary war games. Mama and Daddy never let us play war except when we were visiting their friends whose kids played war. Some kids had real war helmets and cartridge boxes from the war, and they played with toy guns. At one house, the kids had dug holes in the ground. They told us those holes were foxholes. Somehow we knew that a foxhole was supposed to make people safe in war. We never dug our own foxholes, and we didn't play war at home. We never had toy guns either. We had more important things to do at the Brown House than to play war.

A children's version of the Pearl Harbor attack is referenced in "Background Information" at the end of this book.

Eleven

"Hear Dem Bells"

One Sunday morning I was dressed in my blue suit, the one with short pants and a blue jacket and a little blue beanie cap. Mama had combed my hair and sent me outside to "go" while she and the other kids finished getting ready.

At the Brown House we did not have an inside toilet. If we had to "go" at night, we used a large white pail in one of the bedrooms upstairs, usually in the dark. We called it the chamber pot. In cold weather we used the chamber pot even in daytime. In warm weather, we went to the outhouse or some hidden part of the yard, depending on what we needed to do.

We tried to make sure we didn't need to go when we were at church, which was every Sunday morning and every Sunday night and every Wednesday night. The church had just one outhouse, and it always smelled bad. Besides, we didn't want anyone to see us going there. We were always sure to go before we drove to town for church.

Outside on this particular day, the morning was beautiful and quiet. The air was clear and warm, and it felt like a soft, warm blanket covering all the living things in our yard. The large yellow rose bush was in bloom, so I decided to "go" there. As I was doing what I was supposed to do, a faint breeze drifted across the clover field beyond the bush. I could hear a church bell ringing in Graytown a mile away, calling people to church.

Usually we couldn't hear the church bell, but on this special morning the sound of the bell floated over trees and fields, all the way to the yellow rosebush behind the Brown House where I stood. Even though I was a little boy, I knew I had heard something wonderful.

Now that I am grown up, the sound of a church bell reminds me of that beautiful morning and an old song called "Hear Dem Bells." It is one of the famous sacred songs called Negro spirituals, sung by African-American slaves in their dialect in those early times. Here are the words I remember the most.

"Hear dem bells? Don't you hear dem bells?
Dey's a ringin' out da glory ob da Lamb!"

The church bell I heard that morning was ringing out the glory of God, calling people to pray. Like me, the people who heard that church bell were leading lives that were safe in and around that small, pleasant town in Ohio. They had worked hard all week, and they needed this day of worship and rest. They were living in the middle of a great, safe country, and they were free, like me, to go to church and have dinner and take naps and play after church. It was a good time to be alive and a good place to be living.

Many years later, I learned that 1943 was one of the most terrible years of the war. At the very moment I was standing by the rose bush, hearing the church bell in Graytown, other kids like me in other countries were in danger. Their homes were being destroyed, and some of those kids were being made to walk far from home to live in very strange places. Many of those kids lost their toys and books when they had to leave their homes because of the war. Even worse things happened to some of those kids and their families.

I didn't know it then, but one of the worst times of the war was happening right then overseas in a place called Stolp, which is now in the country of Poland. My great-great-grandpa lived there before he came to live in Ohio. If he and his family had stayed in Stolp, my family and I would have been in the middle of the war zone. Our house might have been bombed like many others were.

Many other wars have happened since the war that started when my family and I lived at the Brown House. Even today there are wars in distant lands. These wars cause trouble and difficulties for many people. But church bells are still ringing, calling people to pray, ringing out the glory of the Lamb, and calling out for peace. And those bells are calling us to pray for people in trouble and calling us to do something to help if we can.

World War II damage to my family's town of origin in Prussia is reported briefly in "Background Information" at the end of this book.

Twelve

BROWN SUGAR AND RAISINS

My life at the Brown House was simple in many ways. I had a few toys, and I had time to play. I had Mama and Daddy and my two brothers, and I was only three years old. Mama was always with us. Daddy was usually at work, but he always *seemed* to be with us, even when he was at work. Mama and Daddy worked hard so we boys' lives would be simple and safe.

One day part of our happy life changed. It was a sudden change that came without warning on a very nice, sunny afternoon. I didn't know it, but Mama was about to go to work at the Sun Oil refinery. On this particular day, I found out what that change would mean for me.

I had been playing outside, barefoot as usual, in my short pants. Everything was good. The grass was green, there was cold water from the well, the sky was blue, and it was good to run and yell and imagine things. Someone came to visit, but I didn't pay any attention. She was there to see Mama, not me. I don't remember who this person was, even now, but she seemed like a kind and pleasant lady.

After the lady arrived, I kept playing in the yard until Mama called me into the house. When I came in, she told me that the lady sitting there in our kitchen would be staying with my brothers and me until Daddy came home from work that evening. She said the lady was "the babysitter." It was a new word for me.

Mama then gave me my favorite treat, a little bowl of brown sugar and raisins mixed together, while she talked with the babysitter. I was happy, and I thought this day would be just another good day like every other.

I sat at the table with my bowl of brown sugar and raisins, picking at the treat with my fingers. Mama and the lady talked, and then it was quiet. I took another bite of my brown sugar and raisins, but when I looked out the window toward the road, I saw a frightening sight. The family's black Model A Ford was speeding down the driveway toward the road, followed by a cloud of dust. I knew in an instant that Mama was in the car, and she was leaving me alone with this stranger.

The blackness of the car came over me like a cloud of dread. I felt all alone. I screamed and cried and jumped down from my chair, but the babysitter caught me and put me back in the chair. "It's all right," she said. "Just eat your brown sugar and raisins."

I tried to stop sobbing, but when I reached into the bowl for another bite, I felt something wet on my hand. My tears were falling into my treat! I cried all the harder and pushed the bowl away. All I could think of was that black, black car speeding down the driveway, trailed by a cloud of dust, taking Mama away from me.

I must have stopped crying sometime that day. There must have been some toys to play with so things got better. Daddy came home that evening while we boys were still up, and he played with us before bedtime.

Mama came home sometime that night after I was asleep. All was well in the morning, but times had changed. My life had changed. Mama was going to be working second shift at the refinery for a year, gone from the Brown House in the afternoons and evenings. I never enjoyed my brown sugar and raisins as much after the day Mama first went to work.

Thirteen

Escaping the Babysitter

Even though we had many fun things to do at the Brown House, I was sad for a long time after Mama started going away to work each day. Later I learned that she went to work in "the lab" at the Sun Oil Refinery to help pay for our new house. At the refinery, dirty, black crude oil was "cooked," or refined, to make products for engines. In the lab, the oil and gasoline were tested to make sure they were turning out the way they were supposed to. Mama helped make sure that the gasoline was cooked right so it would work in cars, trucks, and airplanes.

Each time Mama left for work, she arranged for us three boys to have a babysitter. She tried out a few before she found the really good ones. The babysitters mostly were older women, but sometimes they were young women with boyfriends or husbands. Some of them played with us, but some of them just wanted us to behave. Some of them were nice, but not all of them. The ones that were nice were never as nice as Mama.

I got into trouble with babysitters at the Brown House. I remember one especially scary babysitter and her boyfriend. When I woke up from my afternoon nap one day, I saw that Mama was gone and a great big babysitter was sitting at the kitchen table. I had seen her before, and I didn't like her. A man was sitting across the table from her, and they were so busy talking that they didn't see me at first. Then the man saw me, and he said in a gruff voice, "Who's that, Lillian?"

The babysitter spun around and saw me. "Oh, it's just one of *them*," she said. "He musta woke up from his nap." She turned to the big man and they started talking again.

I was hungry after my nap, so I said, "Could I have a cookie now?"

Lillian looked over her shoulder at me. "Cantcha see we're talkin'?" she said in a loud voice. "I'll getcha a cookie later. Now go away!"

I was so surprised that I didn't know what to say. I just stood there looking at them. Then the man did something strange. He pulled a little package out of his pocket and put a white paper roll in his mouth. He struck a match and lit the end of the little paper roll. He sucked in, and soon he blew a cloud of smoke right out of his mouth and even out his nose! It made him seem even scarier.

"Whatcha lookin' at, kid?" he growled. "Hain't ya never seen a man havin' a smoke?"

I couldn't answer. I was so scared.

"G'wan, beat it!" said Lillian the babysitter. "Di'n I tell ya ta git lost?"

I was so scared then that I really did want to get lost. I looked at the other side of the kitchen to the door, the yard, the barn, and the driveway. I wanted to run out and get away. I looked at the mean big people, and I ran right past them for the door. Before they knew what I was doing, I was out in the yard, almost to the driveway. That's when I remembered I didn't have my shoes on. It had snowed, and my feet were freezing cold. I looked down the driveway, thinking about what to do next. All of a sudden, the babysitter and her boyfriend were outside too.

"Hey! You git back in the house!" Lillian yelled. "You ain't sposed to be out here! And look at them feet! No shoes!" The boyfriend just stood by the kitchen door watching. Taking care of us kids wasn't his job, and he knew it.

I was too scared and cold to run any farther, so the babysitter swooped down and picked me up. She carried me into the house. She seemed as big as the barn and as strong as one of Grandpa's cows. I wanted to get away from her and her boyfriend, so I ran into the living room and hid behind my toy box. My heart was pounding and I was about to cry, but the babysitter didn't follow me. I picked up some toys and waited for something better to happen and for the babysitter to go away.

After a while, the boyfriend went away, but the smell of smoke still hung in the kitchen. Mama was angry about it when she came home late that night.

"Has somebody been smoking here?" she demanded when my brothers and I woke up the next morning. "I can tell Lillian was smoking!"

I didn't say anything. I hoped that Mama wouldn't let Lillian come back again. I wished there would never be another babysitter, not ever.

Mama talked to Lillian the next day about the smoke. Mama had told her not to smoke at the house, so the babysitter told Mama it wasn't her but her boyfriend that had been smoking. This made matters even worse, because Mama didn't want her to have boyfriends at our house, especially if they smoked. They might burn the house down or be mean to us kids. After that day, Lillian never came back. I was glad.

Other babysitters came after that one, and they were better. It wasn't long until Mama stopped working at the oil refinery in the city and was with us all the time again. We boys still got into trouble sometimes, but we knew that Mama loved us and would never be mean to us like that one babysitter. And Mama would never tell us to get lost if we asked for a cookie. In fact, we asked for cookies all the time, and Mama never did tell us to get lost.

The term "babysitter" was first used shortly before World War II but became common during the war and later. See "Background Information" at the end of this book.

Fourteen

Going to See the Hole

One day while Mama and Daddy were both away, the babysitter asked us kids if we would like to go to see "the hole." My brothers and I had been there once with Mama, and we knew it was deep and scary. Merl and I remembered and said we wanted to go. Owen was only two years old and didn't even know what a hole was, but he jumped up and down and yelled, "Me, too! Me, too!"

A house had once stood on the other side of Graytown Road. The house had been torn down long ago, but the basement was still there, a large, fascinating hole in the ground. It was better than a regular hole in the ground because it was large and square and had stone walls. We didn't know about ancient ruins, but we could tell that this place was something old and interesting. To us it *was* an ancient ruin. We called it "the hole."

The hole was a long way from our house, at least for those of us who were three years old or younger. To people who lived in town, it would have been the distance of a block or two. Out in the country, it just seemed like a long walk, one we wouldn't dare to take by ourselves.

Owen and I went to the hole only when Merl went, and even Merl couldn't go there without a babysitter or some other really grown up person.

To get to the hole, we had to walk all the way to the end of our white gravel driveway, past the orchard, past the big tall corn and the thistles that could poke us, and all the way to Graytown Road. At the road, we might fall in the ditch, and for sure we had to look both ways lots of times before going across. Cars went very fast on the road.

On this particular day, all three of us boys went to the hole with our babysitter. Eloise and Keithie Freimark were at our house, so they went with us too. Eloise and Keithie were bigger kids who lived a little way down the road. Eloise was even big enough to babysit sometimes, so she must have been about twelve years old. Keithie was about seven or eight, a little older than my big brother Merl. They both seemed pretty big to me.

The day when we went to the hole was hot, and bugs were flying up out of the tall weeds around the hole. "Be very careful!" the big kids said. I wasn't even sure *how* to be careful, so I just tried to do whatever the big kids did.

"Come over here and you can look to the bottom!" Keithie said. We carefully shuffled up to the edge of the concrete foundation and looked down into the hole. Weeds were growing down there, and there were pieces of broken bricks and boards. Someone had thrown in some trash too: broken bottles and old newspapers.

We were cautious as we looked. We didn't want to fall into the hole or climb down in. "There's probably snakes and mice down there," Eloise warned us. I'm not sure if I knew what a snake was at that time, but I could tell by the way she talked that it must be a scary thing.

We walked all around the hole and looked into the scary abyss. It was hard for me to imagine the house that had stood there. Maybe kids like us had lived there. Maybe they were grown up and old now. I was thinking about what that old house might have looked like when the babysitter said, "Okay, kids. Time to go!"

No one argued or asked to stay longer. We had seen enough of the hole for that day, and we wanted to get away from the bugs.

It turned out that our field trip to the hole helped me later when I was in school. There was a story in one of our *Dick and Jane* reading books about a big building going up in a city. The story had pictures of workers digging a deep hole where the building would stand. If I hadn't gone to the hole, I wouldn't have known that a hole was needed to make a big building. When we came to that story in school, I felt lucky that I had been able to see the hole on Graytown Road. For once, I felt I was advanced for my age, more educated than any of the other kids.

The history of Dick and Jane *books is reported briefly in "Background Information" at the end of this book.*

Part Three

MOVING AWAY FROM INNOCENCE

Fifteen

SCARING THE BROWN HOUSE BEAR

Many dangers existed around the Brown House when I lived there. The area of Ohio where it is located was once covered with trees and shallow water, and it was called the Black Swamp. The greatest dangers in the Black Swamp came from animals.

The largest animals were thought to have left the area when the swamp was drained for farming a hundred years earlier. But some of those animals, including bears, seemed nearby, especially after dark. My brothers and I knew a lot about bears from stories such as "Goldilocks and the Three Bears," and "How the Bear Lost His Tail." Bears, we knew, were creatures not to be trifled with.

On this special night, bedtime came as usual. We three boys had had our cookies and milk, because even back then we were quite civilized. It was October, and the weather at night was cool, so it was good to be inside with the windows closed.

My bedroom was at the top of steep, narrow stairs. Mama led the way with one of the kerosene lamps. It was colder the higher we climbed.

Mama helped me into my bed, and I snuggled down under the quilts and prayed with her. The lamp gave a soft yellow light, and it made a cozy, smoky smell. After the prayer, Mama said goodnight. She then took the lamp with her and went back down to tidy up the kitchen.

My brothers were sleeping in another room that night, and this was one of the first nights I was sleeping in a bedroom alone. I wasn't afraid. I didn't anticipate any danger. All I expected was sleep after a busy day of play. But I would soon face one of the greatest dangers of my young life.

Suddenly, in the blackness of that unlit room, I felt my life in danger. I looked as best as I could into the darkness. Dim light from stars marked the window, but there was no moon. Somehow I could feel that a bear was coming. I could sense his presence. I even thought I could smell his oily, matted fur.

Silently I slid up in my bed until I was sitting against my pillow, facing the window. All I could do was watch for the approaching danger. The bear had placed a ladder against the house, I thought, and it was climbing up to my window! My eyes bulged at the horrible sight as its huge black head appeared above the windowsill. For a terrifying moment, I sat facing the bear, expecting it to lunge at me through the window with a loud, scary roar.

But no sound came from the bear. Instead it came from me! I sat up higher in the bed, took a very deep breath, and yelled, "Heyyyyaaaaaah!"

My voice was so strong, so brave, and so ear splitting that the bear disappeared. I had only seen its head, but now it was gone and my room was silent again. All I could hear was my yell, echoing in my ears. I stared at the starry window for a few minutes and confidently slid back under the covers. That bear wouldn't dare come back, knowing he would have to deal with me again.

The next morning, I decided that the bear must have been very scared that night. It had tried to disappear without a trace. My brothers and I couldn't find the bear's ladder or the dents in the lawn where its ladder must have stood. The bear must have smoothed over that place and covered its tracks as it escaped across the fields and into the distant woods. I must have scared him within an inch of his life.

We had no more trouble with bears while we lived at the Brown House. I was glad to have made that part of Ohio safe at night for children.

The historical and current distribution of bears in Ohio is reported in "Background Information" at the end of this book.

Sixteen

Stolen Fudge

This is a story about one of the worst things I did at the Brown House. To me it's almost like the story of the Garden of Eden when the first man and woman ate something they weren't supposed to and got into big trouble.

This happened on Christmas Day 1942. I had turned three in October that year, so I would have been able to do what I'm about to tell you. A year earlier I couldn't have pulled it off, and a year later we no longer lived at the Brown House. We left the Brown House in the summer of 1943, so I know this happened on Christmas Day 1942.

The day was clear, bright, and cold. A sparkling blanket of snow had snuggled in around the corn stubble in the field behind the Brown House, and the house felt especially warm and cozy. A sparkling little Christmas tree stood on a table in the living room. Sunlight poured in the south window, and food smells filled the house. It was good to be alive and three years old.

Sometime late that morning, I heard adult voices in the kitchen. Company had come! We didn't have company often, so I ran to see who the people were and if they had any kids with them. There were no kids, so I kept playing in the living room. The big people came through the kitchen and looked into the living room. They looked all around, saw the Christmas tree and the sunlight, talked among themselves for a minute or two, and then turned back to the kitchen.

Then a strange thing happened. While the group stood looking into the kitchen, a man at the back of the group put his hands behind his back and clasped them there. The man probably was John Johnson, an old Swedish carpenter who went to our church. He had been born in Sweden, and he probably did things like clasping his hands behind his back in the Old Country, but it looked odd and ominous to me. I didn't know about the Old Country, and I wanted to put a stop to it, so I walked over and tried to pull his hands apart. The man jumped when I touched him, and he pulled his hands away.

"Don't hold your hands like that!" I said.

The man raised his bushy eyebrows at me, turned back toward the kitchen, and held his hands behind his back again. Frantically I pulled at his hands to stop this strange thing until one of the visiting ladies saw me and said, "Now don't do that! Don't touch that man!"

The commotion caught Mama's attention. She asked what I had done, and she made me go sit on the couch. I sat on the couch a long time, maybe almost two minutes, my eyes straying around the room. I saw the pretty Christmas tree with presents and toys under it, and I noticed decorations hanging from the ceiling.

This was the year we got the metal cat that held a wooden ball between its front paws and had wheels for hind feet. We could wind the cat up by pumping its metal tail, and it chased the ball. It was also the year we got the small wind-up metal train that sat on a metal base about the size of a dinner plate. The metal base was painted to look like mountains, with a tiny tunnel for the train to go through. A wire held a little airplane above the train, and the airplane flew in circles as the train ran around and around its track.

As I sat there staring at the wrapped presents and wondering what they might be, I saw something else. What was it? A small crockery bowl sat in the sunlight on the window sill at the far end of the room. It was only about a quart size bowl, gray on the bottom and brown on top, with a brown crockery lid. I didn't know what was in it, but it seemed to call out to me. "Nyle!" it whispered, "come here! Look inside."

I glanced toward the kitchen and could tell that the adults had forgotten me. Without making any noise or any sudden moves, I got up and walked smoothly to the crockery bowl. Lifting the lid, I saw brown squares full of nuts, and I smelled something wonderful. I didn't know what it was, so I picked up a piece of it and stuck it in my mouth. It tasted so good that I wanted to wave my arms and run, but instead I walked calmly back to the couch. I bounced a little on the couch, but then I thought that might make people notice me, so I sat very still.

The taste of the soft chocolate and walnuts flooded my mouth. I swirled the first piece in my mouth as it melted, and I looked steadily at the candy bowl across the room. It was still calling me: "Nyle! Come back!"

My senses were overwhelmed by that wonderful flavor. I lost all feeling of my conscience, which usually warned me when I did something that could get me in trouble. Right then I didn't even care about the difference between right and wrong. I didn't feel guilty about what I'd done. I just didn't want to get caught.

Another glance at the kitchen door and another calm walk to the fudge bowl, and I was back on the couch, sucking and chewing the wonderful fudge. Again and again I went to the window and took another piece of fudge each time.

I don't know how many trips I made to the fudge bowl, but I never was caught. Finally I had eaten so much fudge that I thought I might get a stomach ache or be sick and throw up in front of everybody, so I decided to stop. I sat quietly on the couch, innocently swinging my legs. When Mama came back into the living room, she found me sitting there quietly and obediently, as she had told me to do.

"Well! It looks like you are being *especially* good now! How about coming in to the kitchen for some dinner?"

For the first time that day, I felt a little guilty, but I soon got over it.

I followed Mama to the kitchen to have some Christmas food, but the fudge had already satisfied my hunger. We probably had roasted chicken and mashed potatoes and many other good things to eat, but that wonderful fudge and the thrill of having more than my share was all I could think about. It was like the Bible story I'd heard in Sunday school about Adam and Eve eating the forbidden fruit in the Garden of Eden.

The Brown House was like the Garden of Eden to me. That's where I first knew about life, and it was the first place I sinned. Also, like the Garden of Eden, the Brown House was a beautiful place where I can't go again.

Seventeen

LEAKY LUCKY

My older brother, Merl, had an invisible playmate named Leaky Lucky. Leaky Lucky must have become his playmate sometime before I was born, or at least before I was three years old. Merl never told me how Leaky Lucky got his name, and he may not have known. Maybe Leaky Lucky told Merl his name when he first came to play.

Leaky Lucky was a great playmate for Merl. In fact, I'm pretty sure he was a better playmate than I ever was. Leaky Lucky was considerate of Merl and shared his toys nicely. Also, the two of them took turns with the sandbox toys. I have a picture of Merl playing in the sandbox with Leaky Lucky, but you can't see Leaky Lucky in the picture.

Merl was the only one who ever saw Leaky Lucky, but Merl would never say what he looked like. Since Leaky Lucky didn't appear in the picture, I could only guess what he looked like. He was probably a small boy about Merl's age, I thought, and he probably wore about the same clothes as Merl. In the summer, he would have worn short pants and short-sleeved shirts, just like Merl. In the winter, he probably wore snow pants and a plaid cap with earflaps like Merl wore.

Merl needed Leaky Lucky for a playmate because there were no other kids nearby. For three years, Merl was the only child in the family. Even after I was born, I wasn't any fun to play with for a long time. Most of the time, Mama was the only one around the house, and she was usually busy. Leaky Lucky was never busy. He always had time to play, and he was always nice.

Whenever Merl went outside alone to play in the sandbox, Leaky Lucky was there, waiting to play. Merl would sit down in the sandbox and talk with Leaky Lucky about the roads and rivers they were making. When Merl went to the big wooden toy box in the house, Leaky Lucky was there and would let Merl pick out the toys for them to play with. Merl could explain airplanes and trains to his little friend, and he could line up his toys for Leaky Lucky to see. Leaky Lucky always let Merl play with the best toys, but Merl shared nicely too.

Sometimes Leaky Lucky made up games to play with Merl. Nobody knows those games today, but they must have been wonderful. They were probably pirate games and treasure hunts and wild animal hunts. It's too bad Merl can't remember the fun games he and Leaky Lucky played, but he does remember that Leaky Lucky always took the biggest chances in the games, and Merl was always the big boy who helped his friend.

A few times Leaky Lucky got Merl into trouble. He sometimes kept Merl playing too long outside when it was time to come in. Mama would call Merl in for lunch and a nap, and Leaky Lucky would tell Merl to stay and play. When Mama scolded Merl for being late for lunch, Merl told her that it was all Leaky Lucky's fault. That was a safe thing for Merl to say. Leaky Lucky didn't live at our house, so he didn't get into trouble when Merl blamed him.

One time Merl was playing outside in the snow with Leaky Lucky. As the winter clouds darkened in the late afternoon, Mama called Merl to come in for supper. Merl and Leaky Lucky were busy tracking bears in the Black Swamp, so Merl decided they couldn't stop for supper. They kept tracking bears until suddenly something grabbed Merl on the arm. "A bear!" he thought. But before he could scream, he saw it was Mama.

"Merl, why didn't you come in when I called you?" she said.

Merl looked around, but Leaky Lucky was gone. "I was playing with Leaky Lucky. We were looking for a bear."

"Leaky Lucky? Don't blame Leaky Lucky again!" Mama said. "Besides, I don't even see Leaky Lucky's tracks in the snow."

Merl looked around in the snow, and he couldn't see Leaky Lucky's tracks either. There were lots of mysterious things in the world like not seeing Leaky Lucky's tracks in the snow, and Merl probably figured it was just another one of those mysteries.

Telling Merl not to blame Lucky Leaky was the most Mama ever said against Leaky Lucky. She must have laughed quietly about Merl's story. She liked Leaky Lucky and was glad he came to play with Merl except when he caused Merl to be late for supper.

For two or three years, Merl played with Leaky Lucky nearly every day. The two of them were the best of friends. But when I started noticing toys and other things, and when I started crawling and walking on my own, Merl started noticing me. Merl helped me learn to walk, just the way he had helped Leaky Lucky in the dangerous parts of their games.

After I was walking, Merl didn't play with Leaky Lucky so much. He only went outside and played with Leaky Lucky when I was sleeping or sick or in a bad mood. As time went on, Mama noticed Merl played with me more and more and Leaky Lucky less and less.

One day something happened that chased Leaky Lucky away. I had overheard my parents talk to Merl, and all of the sudden, I understood that my brother had a name. I couldn't say "Merl" like my parents did, but that day I tried it when we were playing together. I said, "Muuu-ooo!"

Merl knew immediately that I meant him. He ran to tell Mama. "He said my name! Nyle said 'Merl,' but he didn't say it right!"

Merl was so excited that he ran back to me to have me say "Muuu-ooo" again. He kept trying to get me to talk, and from then on he paid more attention to me than to Leaky Lucky.

After the day when I said "Muuu-ooo!" Leaky Lucky came to play with Merl less and less. Then one day Merl went out to play during my naptime, and Leaky Lucky wasn't there. Merl played by himself and had a good time, but when he went inside, he said to Mama, "Leaky Lucky didn't come today."

Mama smiled and hugged him and said, "He's probably busy now. Maybe he has a baby brother too." What she said reminded Merl of me, so he went to see if I was up from my nap.

Mama didn't mention Leaky Lucky to Merl after that day because she thought it might make Merl sad. But one rainy day several months later, after I had broken one of his toys, Merl said, "I miss Leaky Lucky."

"He hasn't been around for a while, has he?" Mama said. "He probably knows you have been busy."

Merl thought for a minute, and then he smiled and jumped and clapped his hands. "I *have* been busy!" he yelled, "and now I'm going to school!"

"Yes, you are," Mama said. "Your first day in first grade is next Tuesday!"

Just as Mama had said, Merl started first grade in Graytown the next week, and he met lots of big kids, first graders like him. He became very busy reading books and writing numbers. He was good at schoolwork, and he liked school from the very start. When he was at home, I played with him a lot. I was already three years old, and I wasn't such a baby anymore.

When Merl had been in school several weeks, he suddenly remembered that Leaky Lucky was gone. But by then Merl was so grown up that he just felt happy that he had once had such a good friend as Leaky Lucky.

After our family moved to the new house and Merl was in second grade, he said one day, "Mama, what happened to Leaky Lucky? Where is he now?"

Mama thought a minute. "Maybe Leaky Lucky is still a little boy like you were, and maybe he is playing with another little boy who doesn't yet have a baby brother."

Merl felt happy then. Mama was happy too. I'm happy now too whenever I think of Leaky Lucky, even though I never played with him, and even though he went away because of me.

Updated information about Leaky Lucky and other children's imaginary playmates appears in "Background Information" at the end of this book.

Eighteen

TRAGEDY ROARS BY

On the north side of the Brown House was a large open area, paved with white limestone gravel, where big farm trucks and wagons could turn around to load and unload. On the far side of that gravel area was a barn, a machine shed, and other farm buildings. City people might call the gravel area a parking lot or a driveway. Farm people might call it a barnyard. It was a dangerous place when the big trucks or tractors drove through to the barn or the fields.

To us boys it seemed like a long way from the house to the barn, so we seldom walked out onto that great, white graveled space. One day we learned how dangerous it was. My younger brother, Owen, was a toddler when the tragedy almost happened. He must have been about two years old. I don't remember what happened that day. I only remember what I heard about it from Mama long after it happened.

It was a nice summer morning. Mama was busy with housework, and we three boys were playing outside. We always felt safe playing outside at the Brown House. That day was different. For some reason, Owen toddled out onto the great white space of the driveway. Mama didn't know it. She was busy washing clothes. My older brother, Merl, didn't notice where Owen was, either. Merl was busy playing just as I was.

Suddenly a truck came roaring up our long driveway from the road. Mama heard the truck. "Where is Owen?" she shouted out to Merl. "Where is Owen?"

Merl looked up with a blank stare. Before he could answer, Mama ran to the door just in time to see Owen standing in the driveway. The truck was headed straight toward him. "Owen!" she yelled to him and then, "Stop! Stop the truck! Stop!" she screamed as she ran toward the truck.

The driver saw her and slammed on the brakes. The truck skidded to a stop. Owen was on the other side of the truck, and Mama couldn't see him. Thinking the truck had run over him, she screamed and cried as she ran around the truck. One of the men jumped from the truck and picked Owen up. When Mama saw that, she thought Owen must be badly hurt or killed. Mama kept screaming and crying until she found that he wasn't even hurt. Owen wasn't very scared until he heard Mama crying, and then he cried too.

Merl came running, and Merl and I cried too. The men who were in the truck all gathered around, and some of them cried too. Some of them looked to the sky and said, "Gracias a Dios!"

Mama cried more, since she knew what those words meant. She said, "Yes, thank you, God!"

The truck had been bringing men we called Mexicans to work in the nearby tomato fields. We called them Mexicans because they spoke Spanish, but they probably were from Texas. Many came each year to help plant tomatoes, pickles, and sugar beets. Later each year they helped harvest those crops.

After they found out Owen was okay, the Mexicans talked Spanish among themselves. Those who knew some English talked to Mama and said they were sorry. She said it wasn't their fault and that everything was okay. They picked up their work things, went around the barn, walked out into the field to pick tomatoes.

Mama took Owen into the house and sat him down on the kitchen floor. She cried again, and Merl and I came to see what was wrong. She hugged all of us, and we all cried, but we boys didn't know why we were crying. Mama was crying, so we did too. Soon it was all over. Then we all went back to our work and play. When Daddy came home from work and Mama told him what had happened, he cried too.

For many, many years, Mama told us about that day. She would look up from her work and shudder when she remembered it, and sometimes she would cry. Sometimes she told us how thankful she was that day, and we were thankful too because Mama was thankful and we were all thankful that Owen wasn't hurt.

Migratory work during World War II and the subsequent mechanization of agriculture are reported briefly in "Background Information" at the end of this book.

Nineteen

RIDING THE TOMATO PLANTER

In the summer, thousands of tomatoes grew in the fields around the Brown House. The tomatoes were raised by local farmers, mainly for canning in a nearby factory. At the factory they were made into ketchup, tomato sauce, tomato paste, crushed tomatoes, and just plain canned tomatoes. They were not made into pizza sauce because no one in Ohio had heard of pizza in those days, and we had barely heard of spaghetti.

The tomatoes were good to eat right off the vine, and the farmers never cared if my brothers and I picked a few to eat. We liked to go out into the fields, pick a few tomatoes that looked good, wipe the dirt off on our shirts, and eat them like apples.

Late in the spring, tomato plants were set into the ground in long rows when the weather was warm enough. The plants had to be started in greenhouses much earlier in the spring, and then they were planted in the fields when they were only a few inches tall. They had to be placed in the ground very carefully by hand, and they had to be placed a certain distance apart. If they were too close to each other, they would get crowded and wouldn't grow as well. If they were planted too far apart, there would be fewer tomatoes.

It was a big job for the Mexicans who worked in the fields to plant so many tomato seedlings by hand, but the process was made much easier using a machine called a tomato planter. The tomato planter was a piece of farm equipment that was pulled through the fields either by a team of horses or a farm tractor. It had big metal wheels and a low bench on each side, where workers sat near the ground to set the tomatoes onto the soil. Small shovels like small snowplows were attached to the front of the tomato planter on each side.

As the planter was pulled through the field, the shovels dug small valleys in the dirt about four inches deep, just deep enough for the small plants. People riding on benches on each side placed plants in the ground at the correct distance from each other. Other little shovels at the back of the tomato planter then pushed dirt in from both sides to close the valley so the roots were covered and the plants could grow.

We kids never rode the tomato planter out in the field. We never planted tomatoes from the machine. We only rode the tomato planter when it was standing still in the barn. It was fun to go in the barn on a hot summer day. It was cool inside, and the musty, dusty smell of the barn smelled like fun to us. We took turns sitting on the tomato planter's low benches near the ground, and we pretended to plant tomatoes. Mainly we pretended to be taking a ride. Sometimes we would roll off onto the barn floor, pretending to be falling from the machine out in the field.

We thought it would be fun to ride the planter through the fields, but we had no idea how hard the Mexicans worked. It was cool and shady in the barn when we rode the tomato planter, but it was usually hot, humid, and sunny when the Mexicans planted tomatoes.

Besides planting tomatoes, there were lots of other grown-up things we kids liked to pretend to do, such as painting the house, giving haircuts, hunting animals, or fixing cars. Sometimes it was more fun to pretend to do grown-up work than to play with our toys. Years later we grew up and did some of the same jobs that we had played at as children.

It was good that we had seen big people doing grown-up work while we were little. When we were older, we could see the difference between pretending and actually doing real work. Both pretending and really working are good. Which one you do just depends on how old you are and what needs to be done. Sometimes you need to work, and sometimes it's more important to play.

A short video of a modern tomato planter in operation is referenced in "Background Information" at the end of this book.

Twenty

THE PEAR

Mama and Uncle Harris were in the front seat of my uncle's car, and they were talking grown-up talk. My brother Owen and I were in the back seat, bouncing up and down and talking about things that seemed real to us. In 1943 kids didn't have to sit in car seats and people didn't have to wear seatbelts. Nobody even *had* seatbelts then. So we were free to bounce and play in the backseat of the car.

We were on our way home from Grandma's house, where we had played while Uncle Harris and Mama were shopping in Fremont and Daddy was at work.

At Grandma's house we always had fun. We could run on the sidewalk out to the milk house and stick our hands into the cold water around the milk cans. We could chase the chickens around the yard and get feathers from them. Sometimes we could get chicken poop between our toes if we were barefoot in summertime. Sometimes we could see Grandpa milk the cows at the barn. Today Uncle Harris and Mama had come back too soon, so there wasn't time to help Grandpa with the chores.

The Pear

When Mama asked how we had been while she was gone, Grandma told her that we had been good boys even though Owen had cried when he fell down on the stones. Mama was glad to hear the news and didn't seem concerned about Owen's fall. She told us to get our coats, so we got them, buttoned up, and climbed into the back seat of Uncle Harris's car.

Mama and Uncle Harris had started talking grown-up talk as soon as we left Grandma's house. Pretty soon, Uncle Harris said, "You boys know what's in the trunk?"

We didn't know he was talking to us until Mama turned around and said, "What do you think is in the trunk? It's something for you boys."

I started thinking about what I wanted. Maybe it was a red toy. I didn't know the name of the toy, but I wanted it to be red. Or maybe there was a whole box of toys in the trunk. "What is it?" I asked finally and looked at Owen. He was thinking about a whole box of toys too. I could tell.

Uncle Harris laughed. He said, "I'll tell you what it is. It's a pair!"

Owen and I didn't say anything. We couldn't remember what a pear was.

"You know what a pear is, don't you?" Mama said and laughed.

Then I remembered. Pears were things like apples that fell off the tree in Grandma's yard and were all squishy if we fell down on them. We liked to throw the hard ones at the tree, but we weren't supposed to do that.

But why was the pear in the trunk? I wondered. Oh! It must be huge, the size of the trunk of Uncle Harris's car! We could make a pumpkin face from it and maybe even get inside it like Peter, Peter, Pumpkin Eater! But how did Uncle Harris get such a giant pear into the trunk, and how would he get it out?

"Is it really a pear?" I asked, letting my imagination run wild.

"How big is it?" Owen yelled, almost screaming because he was so excited. He started jumping up and down just like a baby.

I was afraid Uncle Harris would think I was a baby too, so I grabbed Owen and made him stop jumping up and down. Then, for no reason, Owen hit me. I pushed him away, and he fell on the floor of the car. Then I fell on the floor on top of him. He hit me again, and then he started crying again like a baby, for no reason, I thought. So I hit him. I didn't want to be a baby, and I didn't want him to be one either.

"You two quit that if you want to see the surprise in the trunk!" Mama warned us. We were almost to the Brown House by this time, and we didn't want to lose the surprise. So we wiped our noses and stood up, looking over the top of the front seat until we were home.

When at last we stopped in front of the Brown House, I opened the door, jumped out, and ran back to the trunk.

"What is it, really?" I yelled to Uncle Harris as he came to the back of the car.

"It's a pair. You'll see in a minute," Uncle Harris said as he fumbled with the keys in his hands, looking for the right one to unlock the trunk. Finally he picked one out and opened the trunk. I was excited to see what I thought would be the biggest pear in the world. But nothing was in the trunk except a big cardboard box.

"See, there's no pear!" I yelled, thinking I had been right all along. "There's no pear, is there?" I said, trying not to cry like a baby. I wanted to hit Uncle Harris's car for not having a pear, but I had to act nice or I wouldn't get anything, whatever it was.

"The *pair's* in the box," Uncle Harris said, emphasizing the word *pair* and pulling the box up close. To my complete surprise, he reached inside the box and pulled out two furry little animals.

"Here's the pair!" he said loudly. He laughed and laughed. "It's a pair of doggies!"

Uncle Harris kept laughing as he pushed the dogs at me, but I didn't laugh. I jumped to the side of the car before those furry things could get me. I had never been around dogs, but I knew they had sharp teeth and loved to bite little boys and make loud scary noises that made boys run away.

I stayed far enough away so they couldn't scare me if they made a big noise. I didn't know dogs were ever that small or moved that fast. I watched as they jumped around, too fast for me. "Where's the pear?" I asked very quietly, never taking my eyes from the dogs. "I want a pear."

"This *is* the pair! It's a *pair* of puppies!" Uncle Harris said and laughed some more.

I didn't know many big words, and I usually didn't know why big people laughed, so I didn't know what to do. I was too young to understand the two different words that sound the same: a pear that is a fruit and a pair that is two of something, like a pair of puppies. All I knew was that Uncle Harris was trying to give us two mean little animals and no pear. I didn't understand that he had been joking with us.

Uncle Harris put the two dogs down in the driveway. Owen just walked right over to the dogs. Little kids don't have much sense, I thought. I watched to see what would happen next. He reached down to one of the puppies and said, "Kitty, kitty!"

One dog bit Owen's hand, and the other one jumped up and tried to bite his ear. He screamed and ran toward the house, and the dogs chased him all the way to the door. Getting his body in between the screen door and the big door, he kicked at the dogs through the opening. The dogs yelped. They couldn't get Owen, so they came running back to me at the car.

Mama had gathered her packages from the car, and she hurried with them to help Owen get into the house. The dogs ran after her and started biting at her feet. She kicked at them and scared them away. "Those dogs are pretty wild, Harris," she said.

"Yup," he said, smiling. "These boys gotta play with 'em and tame 'em."

What he said made sense to me, so I thought I would start to tame them right away. I held out my hand to one of them, and he jumped up and bit me. His teeth were sharper than anything! I put my hands over my head, and then both dogs started jumping up and trying to bite them. When I reached down to push them away, one of them bit the arm of my coat. The other one bit the end of my pants.

That was enough for me. I ran for the house, and they came after me, trying to bite me more. I just barely made into the house and shut the screen door. But I watched to see what they would do next.

The two dogs ran around the yard, smelling the grass. Then, right when I was watching, one of them lifted a back leg and did something naughty against the fence. Then the other dog did the same. This was too awful to tell to Owen or Mama, so I just watched them. I wondered if I could ever go outside to play again.

Mama came to the screen door where I was watching the dogs. "Thanks for the ride, Harris," she called out. Uncle Harris just waved as he climbed into his car. Without even looking to see what the dogs were doing, he drove down the lane, onto the road, and was gone.

"Maybe Merl will be able to play with those pups when he comes home from school," Mama said. "They need to be played with to get tame. Merl may be able to do it."

Owen didn't say anything. I didn't say anything. We just took the blocks and the wind-up train and waited for Merl to come home from school. We didn't plan to go outside ever again.

Merl tried to tame that pair of dogs, and so did Mama and Daddy, but those two dogs were never tame enough for us kids to play with. Mama and Daddy eventually sent them away to live with another family and bite their kids instead of us.

Twenty One

LEAVING THE BROWN HOUSE

My family moved out of the Brown House in July 1943. The new house we moved into was twenty-seven years old, but it was new to us. It was less than two miles straight south of the Brown House on the very same road. It was the first house Mama and Daddy ever owned. It was also the only house they ever owned. They lived in it fifty-one years.

I don't remember anything about getting ready to leave the Brown House. I didn't pay attention to the work the big people were doing. All I had to do was stay out of their way and play with my toys. I didn't notice when they took the living room chairs away, when the kitchen table was gone, or when the couch disappeared. Then the beds and blankets were gone, and I didn't see them leave either.

Mama and Daddy and all of my aunts and uncles were busy taking loads and loads of furniture, dishes, pans, blankets, lamps, and everything else to a trailer outside. All of the sudden, I couldn't find my toys.

"Want your toys?" Daddy chuckled when he noticed the look on my face.

"Yeah, I can't find them," I said.

"Come on out here," Daddy said, pushing open the screen door and pointing to the driveway. There in the driveway was our black car and a trailer piled high with chairs and furniture and our toys on the top. "There's your toys!" Daddy said. "Want to ride with them to the new house?"

Merl was already in the trailer, snuggled down among our toys and some of the furniture and boxes. Owen and I wanted to get on the trailer too.

"We've just got room for two more boys!" Daddy said, and he laughed again. He was very happy. He lifted me up into the trailer and set me down into a little hole just big enough for me to stand in. The sides of the trailer came up almost to my shoulders. Daddy lifted Owen into another corner of the trailer, and he was still laughing. It must have been one of the happiest days of his life.

We three brothers looked down at the ground far below us. We looked up at the pile of toys and chairs around us. Finally we looked back at the Brown House. We didn't feel sad, because it seemed we would soon be back. We had always been there, and it seemed we always would be at the Brown House.

"Hold on to the load!" Daddy yelled, laughing again. "Hold onto your toys!"

Slowly we rode down the gravel lane and out to the road. The Brown House and its trees and barns became smaller and smaller as we watched. We turned onto Graytown Road and went slowly around all of the potholes. All three of us boys held our arms out over the load of toys, keeping them safe until we could play with them at our new house. The wind blew past us, and it felt fresh and new. When we remembered to look back, we couldn't see the Brown House at all.

We traveled only about two miles, but it seemed like a long trip. At the new house, the trailer was unloaded somehow. I don't remember that part, because I was still three years old, and big people took care of big things like moving in. We didn't know then that we would never be in the Brown House again. We didn't know how many memories we had brought with us and how we would love those memories forever. The Brown House was where we first knew that we were alive and free and in this world. We always liked stories about the Brown House. That's why I wrote these stories for you.

At our new house there were many new adventures, and we learned about many exciting things that had happened nearby many years earlier when our Daddy was a little boy. He told us stories about fun times and storms and dangers and getting into trouble. But those stories will have to wait for another time.

Part Four

SAMPLE STORIES FROM *LEATHERPORT TALES*

Sample Stories from *Leatherport Tales*

My family moved from the Brown House to a house two miles south on the same country road about three months before my fourth birthday. The new house was in an area known as Leatherport, a place that now seems nearly mythical to me. I heard stories about events that happened there many years earlier, and I had adventures of my own during my years in Leatherport.

The stories that follow are a sampling from my forthcoming collection entitled Leatherport Tales. *"The New House" and "Leatherport" provide background information about the house and the area itself, setting the stage for "The Riding Pig" and "The Calfy Pail," stories that are typical of the entire collection, available in print in 2016.*

The New House

The house my family and I moved into after leaving the Brown House was already twenty-seven years old, but it was a new house to us. My brothers and I missed living at the Brown House, but we somehow knew that our adventures of growing up in the country were not over.

At the new house, tall maple trees gave us shade in the summer and lots of leaves in the fall to play in. The orchard on the north side of the house had twelve kinds of apples, two kinds of pears, a sweet cherry tree, a plum tree, and two apricot trees. Later Daddy planted grape vines in it. He also grafted both apple and pear branches onto one special tree. After a few years, we could pick five kinds of apples and two kinds of pears from just that one tree.

Best of all, it seemed to me, was the pond that bordered our yard on the south and west sides. It was about five acres in area when we arrived. The pond had clear blue water in the middle, floating moss near the shore, and tall cattails at the very edge. Bullfrogs hid among the cattails and jumped under the moss when anyone came near. At night the big bullfrogs "kerjugged" in loud, low voices while smaller frogs chirped in high-pitched, softer voices. Turtles crawled up onto logs at the edge of the water to sun themselves on hot afternoons, and they slid off to hiding places under the moss if I tried to catch them. Redwing blackbirds made nests in the cattails, and tall cranes waded in shallow water to catch fish. Daddy built a flat-bottom boat from marine plywood that was light enough for us young kids to row or pole around the pond. It was a child's paradise, and it was all ours.

Uncle George once owned a brick and field tile factory next door to our new house. He built the foundation and walls of our house in 1916 using large, red tile blocks made in his factory. The tile blocks were about three times the size of regular red bricks but hollow inside for better insulation. He covered the roof with gray slate, thin slices of stone that made a very permanent roof. We didn't call it the red and grey house, but we could have.

The pond at our new house was created when Uncle George's factory workers dug up clay for use in making brick and tile. The men scraped the clay up from the ground with a hand-held scraper pulled by horses or a tractor. They loaded it into cars on the small factory railroad track that ran along the bottom of the clay pit and then pulled the cars to the factory. Steam-powered presses formed the clay into bricks and tile. The tiles and brick were taken outside and dried in the sun until they were ready to be baked in the factory's ovens, called kilns. The coal fires that fueled the kilns created tremendous heat and clouds of smoke that were visible from two or three miles away.

I would have liked to have seen those great kilns and their smoke signals in the sky, but Uncle George shut down the factory eight years before we moved into our new house. The machinery was hauled away, and the buildings were demolished. All that remained were a few foundations and four arched brick kilns where fires once blazed. Sometimes I walked around the abandoned area, just looking for bolts, pieces of iron and coal, and any other remnants of its glorious past.

Our new house had most of the modern comforts of houses available in 1943. It had electric lights, running water, and a flush toilet, things we didn't have at the Brown House. When the house was built in 1916, the lights and heat were provided by natural gas from a gas well behind the big pond. By the time we moved there, the gas pipes and fixtures were gone. Instead, electricity provided lights, and we had a shiny red coal-burning stove for the heat. The indoor toilet was good too so we didn't have to go outside to an outhouse in freezing cold weather.

When we first moved in, we had to cool our food with huge blocks of ice in a wooden icebox on the back porch. Mama also did laundry on the back porch with a washing machine powered by a noisy, smelly gasoline engine. Soon we had an electric refrigerator and an electric washing machine. Later we removed the kerosene kitchen stove and its mysterious blue flames and bought an electric stove that cooked food on beautiful, red-hot electric coils.

Besides all of those nice things about the new house, we liked living closer to family. My elderly Great Uncle George and Great Aunt Mary lived right next door, and Grandpa and Grandma lived on a farm only a half mile away. Aunt Mary gave us kids dried apples, dried pears, and sassafras tea. At the farm we got milk and eggs, fresh from the animals that produced them. We were close enough that we could even walk to Grandpa and Grandma's farm. It seemed to me that we had moved to the very center of our family's world.

With the pond, the orchard, and the big yard, our new home was an even bigger and better Garden of Eden for us kids than the Brown House had been. Another collection of stories will tell about life in and around Leatherport. Some of those stories happened even before my parents were born. Some stories happened after we moved to the new house. Most of those stories will have to be told some other time.

Leatherport

The area where we moved was called Leatherport. It was named after a small settlement that once stood on the Portage River about a mile south of our house. Leatherport settlement was started in 1835 as a trading post when northwestern Ohio was first being occupied by Europeans. Not long after the settlement was started, a leather tanner set up a shop there. Soon a shoe maker, a blacksmith, and a tavern keeper joined him. Those four businessmen decided they should give the place a name, and they named it Leatherport in honor of the leather tanner who owned its first business.

Leatherport was located as far upstream on the Portage River as boats from Lake Erie could travel. Three miles farther upstream was a small town called Elmore, started in 1851. At Elmore the river was shallow, and the exposed limestone bedrock made a perfect place for a railroad bridge. The first railroad bridge to cross the Portage River was built in 1852 in Elmore.

From then on, Leatherport's days were numbered. The settlement had not grown big enough to be called a town, and as Elmore grew due to the railroad, the few people who lived in Leatherport moved away. Eventually no one lived there anymore. Even though the settlement is no longer there, my family and lots of other people still call the area Leatherport.

Across the small pond from our house was a separate half-acre lot that Mama and Daddy bought from Uncle George when they bought the house. Many years earlier, Uncle George's father had loaned that half-acre lot to Harris Township for use as a school for the kids living on nearby farms. In honor of Leatherport, the one-room school was called The Leatherport School. The school became the most lasting legacy of Leatherport settlement.

Grandma and Grandpa Kardatzke went to school in The Leatherport School in the 1890s. Daddy and his brothers and sisters, all nine of them, also started school in that building. Grandma told us kids that the maple trees in the old schoolyard were already big when she started school there in 1889. More than a hundred years later, some of those old giant trees are still there.

The school sat on the east side of Uncle George's tile factory, and clouds of black smoke blew through the schoolyard. As a young mother, Grandma was worried that smoke from the tile factory would be unhealthy for her children when they were old enough to go to school. She insisted that the school building be moved away from the smoke before her first child, my Uncle Harris, started school. So in 1908, the schoolhouse was jacked up on logs, rolled a half mile down the road, and placed in a field across the road from Grandma and Grandpa's house, where no smoke could threaten the health of school children. The new location was even closer to where Leatherport settlement had been, and the school kept its name as The Leatherport School.

After the schoolhouse was moved, Harris Township gave the original schoolyard back to Uncle George. It became part of the property that Mama and Daddy bought from Uncle George in 1943. What a delightful place that land was for all the kids in the area! We kids called it "the park," and that's really what it was. Our church had Sunday school picnics there, and we played crude versions of baseball and football there.

Daddy built a ride in the park that we called "the trolley"—what modern kids would call a zip line. The trolley was a heavy steel cable suspended between two tall maple trees. A pulley hung upside down on the cable, and below the pulley was a swing seat just wide enough for one rider. A rope attached to the pulley allowed one or more kids to pull someone in the seat high up the cable to the tree at one end. When the rope was let go, the rider went whizzing down the cable and back up to a stop high in the other tree. We kids could have made some serious money if we had collected fees for riding the trolley. We never charged for rides, and the trolley became a beloved local landmark.

THE RIDING PIG

"Let's go to Grandpa's house and get some milk," said Daddy one summer evening.

"Okay! Okay! Let's go!" my brother and I yelled. We always liked to go to Grandpa's house, no matter what the errand was. Grandpa's house was an adventure every time for me at age four and my younger brother at three. Even though Grandpa and Grandma lived only a half-mile down the road from us, it was a big trip for kids our age.

When Daddy called us to say it was time to go, my brother Owen and I ran straight for the car. As we clambered into the back seat of our black Model-A Ford car, Daddy said, "Now who would like to ride the riding pig today?"

"I want to! I want to!" Owen and I both yelled.

Grandpa had about a dozen cows, so he had plenty of milk to sell. Going there to get fresh milk for our family was something we did several times a week. Grandpa milked the cows by hand into large metal pails, and we would be going right at milking time. Today, however, we wanted more than just getting milk.

Grandpa treated one pig as a pet even though it lived in the barn-yard with the cows, chickens, and other pigs. Because Grandpa petted it and talked to it, the pig had become so tame that he said a small boy could ride on its back. We had seen the riding pig, but we hadn't ridden her yet. Riding a pig sounded like wonderful fun.

We were excited as we jumped out of the car in front of Grandpa's big red barn. It was dark as we walked through the largest part of the barn, but we could see a light at the back in the milking shed. We loved the barn's smell of hay and animals. We liked to see the cats and chickens that were sometimes hiding inside the barn and the birds that made nests up high. When we reached the milking shed in the back part of the barn, Grandpa was in there, milking cows just as we thought.

"Well! You brought your helpers!" he said and laughed as he saw us. We boys felt good that Grandpa noticed us and called us helpers. It made us feel bigger and more important than we were.

Grandpa brought two foaming pails of warm milk to the door where we were standing. He set the pails down and looked us over, smiling like Santa Claus with his rosy cheeks.

"We wondered if we could get some milk," Daddy said, "and the boys wondered if they could ride the pet pig."

"Shore can," Grandpa said. "I got plenty 'a milk, and I just seen that pig. Let me get these cows outta here first."

Grandpa walked along in front of the cows' heads at the long feed trough. Their heads were clamped between metal bars called stanchions that made them stand still while they were being milked. One by one he unlocked the stanchions. Each huge, ponderous cow backed out of its stall, lumbered to the door, and went out into the muddy back barnyard. When the last cow left, Grandpa went to the door and looked for the pet pig among the other pigs and the cows. It was on the other side of the barnyard, so he called to it.

"Whooo, pig! Whoooeee, pig!" he called in his loud voice.

The pet pig raised her head from where she was rooting. She was glad to see Grandpa because he was her pal. She jumped in the air, squealed with delight, and ran toward the four of us. Pigs have a strange, bucking way of running when they try to run fast. We all laughed to see a pig running to us like a pet dog.

"She's really ready to play," Grandpa said as the pig came to him. She stood still while he patted her. "Now who'll be the first to ride? How about the little guy first?"

Without another word, Grandpa picked up Owen and lifted him above the pig. The pig stood still, sniffing the ground where the cows had just passed through. Slowly and carefully, Grandpa lowered Owen onto the pig's back.

Knowing I would be next, I watched carefully. I could see that the riding pig's back was rounded like that of any other pig, so there was really no place to sit safely and also no way to hang on.

In case you don't know much about pigs, their backs are not flat like the backs of horses and cows. Pigs' backs are rounded, probably because they spend most of their time with their noses on the ground, rooting and digging for disgusting little things they find to eat like roots, seeds, bugs, and food dropped by other animals. Pigs also have powerful necks, and they can lift heavy things with their noses, including sometimes the fences that are supposed to keep them in. Pigs are good at digging under fences or lifting them up with their noses so they can escape.

Owen and I were about to find out that any place we sat on the pig's back made us feel like we were about to fall off. If we sat too far forward, we were likely to fall over the pig's head, right where she is going to walk. If we sat too far back, we might fall off the other end, and you don't want to land at that end of a pig.

As Grandpa lowered Owen onto the pig's back, Owen was scared. "Don't let go, Grandpa! Don't let go!" he yelled.

Grandpa held Owen on the pig's back and nudged the pig to make her take a few steps. She moved, and all the time, Owen kept making scaredy-cat noises, and I could tell he was about ready to cry.

I was bigger, so I knew I wouldn't be scared when it was my turn. I couldn't wait for Owen to get off the pig so I could ride. I could see what he was doing wrong too. He was sitting too near the pig's head, so he was about to fall off the front. He wasn't putting his hands on the pig's back to keep from falling forward, and he didn't have his feet squeezed against the pig's sides to hang on. I would do everything differently, and I would make the pig give me a good ride, maybe all around the barnyard and back to Grandpa.

"Put me on now, Grandpa!" I said as he lifted Owen off. "I want a bigger ride! I know how to ride the pig!" I shouted.

"Oh you do, do you?" Grandpa said, laughing. "How do you know?"

"I was watching," I said.

"Okay, here you go!" he said as he picked me up and started to put me right where Owen had been sitting.

"Not there, Grandpa," I said. "Put me farther back. Put me right at the top."

"How's that?" Grandpa asked after he had settled me at the very top of the pig's arched back.

"Okay, Grandpa, okay!" I said breathlessly. "Let me go now. I can ride by myself."

Grandpa was chuckling as he let go of me and stepped back. Meanwhile the pig, with me aboard, was just standing in the doorway of the milking shed, looking out into the barnyard. I wanted the pig to go forward so I could have my big ride. I knew just what to do.

Everybody was quiet and watching as I squeezed my knees and feet against the pig's sides. I leaned forward a little so I could put my hands on the pig's back for balance, and then I gave a little kick with my feet and rocked back and forth to make the pig move. In response, the pig took a couple of steps forward into the muddy barnyard. I was doing it! I was riding the pig! Everybody behind me laughed and cheered.

After taking those few steps into the mud and manure in the barnyard, the pig stopped and looked around. She was probably pleased with what she saw. It was a warm, friendly barnyard, filled with pig-friends, slow-moving cow-friends, and busy chicken-friends. Suddenly the riding pig saw her favorite cow doing something across the barnyard. The other pigs saw it too, and pigs everywhere squealed and began to run.

The next thing I knew, something very bad happened. It was so bad that I will remember it always. The riding pig let out a scream of excitement. "Arrreeeeeuuuuuh!" she shrieked and burst forward so fast that she shot out from under me. I fell straight down. Splat! Into the mud and manure. I looked up just in time to see that the riding pig had won the race across the barnyard. What a fast pig!

Grandpa laughed, Daddy laughed, and Owen laughed. They laughed so hard they couldn't breathe. Everybody was laughing except me. I was angry because they were laughing, but I was proud that I had almost ridden the riding pig across the barnyard just as I had dreamed I might.

I picked myself up from the muddy manure and knocked as much of it off as I could, but there was still mud on the seat of my pants that wouldn't knock off.

"What happened?" Grandpa asked, laughing so hard he was choking for breath. "What happened?" he asked again and then added with another guffaw, "Did the pig throw you off?"

Daddy spoke next. "I guess that was a *bucking* pig, and she threw you off!"

That comment really made me angry. The pig didn't throw me off. I was riding just fine until she ran out from under me.

"Nope," I muttered in defense, brushing my pants again. "The pig just ran away!"

I didn't look up at Grandpa or Daddy or Owen. Burning with embarrassment, I walked right past them and into the barn. They all laughed again and followed me.

At the milk house, Grandpa filled our one-gallon jars with fresh milk. He poured the rest of the milk into a large metal milk can that stood in cold water in a pit in the milk house floor. The milk truck would come the next day and take two or three of those big cans of milk to town. From there a train would take the milk to a big city, maybe Toledo or Fremont, so city kids could have milk on their corn flakes just like us.

After everyone was done laughing and talking about my ride on the pig, we walked back to the car. Daddy and Owen climbed in.

"You better stand up," Daddy said to me, "so you don't get dirt on the seat." So I climbed in and stood, holding onto the front seat, until we arrived at our house.

"I'll never ride another pig," I said to myself. And I never did.

THE CALFY PAIL

This is the first story I remember hearing from my father, who liked to begin his story telling with "when Daddy was a little boy." I heard it from my father when I was very young, and I asked him to retell it many times. When I became a father, I told the story to my children. It made me want to remember some of the other things that happened when I was a boy so I would have stories to tell my children.

"Why is Ted running up the yard?" Ma asked. "Better check, Arlin."

Arlin sprang to the door. Sure enough, his cousin Ted was running right up to the house.

"They're draining the pond!" Ted yelled. "The ditch is running like a river!"

Arlin looked at Ma. "Can I go see? I already shelled the corn for the chickens."

"Pa give you any other chores?" asked Ma.

Arlin shook his head no.

"Okay. But you boys don't go a gittin' drownded! We don't need none of that!"

The two boys ran across the yard and onto the road before anyone could call for them to help with something. They didn't want anything to spoil this great time for play. The sun had come out and was warming the dry grass along the ditch bank beside the road. The air was cool, but the sun made it feel that summer was coming, filled with good things like going barefoot, catching frogs, swimming, and freezing ice cream.

When Ted and Arlin reached the ditch, they could see deep water flowing down from the pond at the brick and tile factory about a half mile up the road. The land where they stood was perfectly flat, so they knew a flooded ditch wasn't natural. It was man-made. Uncle George Gleckler was pumping water from the tile factory pond so he could re-start the brick and tile factory for another season. He dug up tons of clay to be pressed into bricks and into foot-long cylindrical tiles that were being laid by the thousands under farm fields to drain them. It was the factory's enormous pump house that was creating this artificial torrent.

The boys watched the muddy water push its way down the ditch, past the barn, under the driveway through the culvert, past the lawn and the house, and finally into the mouth of the large tunnel, called a drain tile, that carried the water underneath the fields for a quarter of a mile to the Portage River. The mouth of the drain tile, which was about two and a half feet in diameter, was mysterious and scary, even when the ditch was not flooded. But now it looked like the open mouth of a monster or a serpent, swallowing up the ditch water and anyone who came too near. Arlin and Ted didn't plan to play anywhere near that dangerous tunnel.

The rushing water made Arlin think. "I have an idea!" he said.

Arlin was looking toward the ditch, with its dark, swirling water. Ted looked at the ditch too, but he didn't have an idea.

"What?" Ted asked.

"Let's play boats!" Arlin yelled.

Ted looked at the ditch again and remembered hearing about a boy in their class who had drowned while playing in a creek near town. The ditch wasn't as big as the creek, but there was probably enough water to drown an eight-year-old boy. Besides, the water was cold and muddy, and he especially didn't want to drown in cold, muddy water.

"I ain't goin' in no boat in no muddy ditch today!" Ted said.

"No! Not real boats! Play boats!" Arlin said. "Let's find boats to float down the ditch!"

This idea was much better, but Ted couldn't think of any boats they had. Arlin was a little older, so he sometimes could think of things sooner.

"Where we going to get boats?" Ted asked cautiously.

"Let's go look in the barn," Arlin suggested. "There's gotta be something there we can float down the ditch."

The boys ran over to the big red barn. Now that Ted thought of it, he realized that at least one fine boat had to be in the big barn somewhere, maybe more. He was right. Just inside the door, there it was. Well, it wasn't exactly a boat, but it would be fun to float in the ditch.

Both boys saw it at once, and Arlin said, "Yes, sir, there's our boat!"

"Yeah!" Ted yelled, but then he fell silent with a sad, dark thought. "Isn't that the calfy pail?"

"Sure, it's the calfy pail, but so what?" Arlin said, taking it from its hook on the wall.

"I thought you were never supposed to play with the calfy pail," Ted replied, almost whispering now. "I heard your Pa say you could play with almost anything around the barn, but you should never touch the calfy pail."

Arlin knew Ted was right. He thought for a minute about what Pa had said, and he looked at the calfy pail again. The pail was special because it had a rubber nipple coming out its side near the bottom. The pail was used for feeding milk to young calves that needed more milk than their mother cows could provide. The calfy pail served as a baby bottle for them. Without the calfy pail, the three young calves right now in the barn would not be able to get enough milk.

Arlin thought for a minute. Pa would need the calfy pail at milking time that night, but that was a long way off. Besides, he was a bigger boy now than when Pa had said not to play with it. He could be extra careful now that he was so big.

"Pa said that when I was just little. I think I can be careful enough now," Arlin said. He lifted the pail from the hook, and the two boys left the barn through the back door, where they wouldn't be seen from the house.

As they walked, the two boys planned that one of them would take the pail upstream some distance and float it down to the other boy like a boat. That boy would grab it from the fast-moving ditch water. They then would trade places and sail the boat down the flooded ditch again.

Arlin took the first turn, running up the ditch a good long way. He carefully set the pail in the water and watched it float down to Ted. Ted stepped carefully down the steep ditch bank, reached out, and grabbed the handle. He then ran upstream while Arlin ran downstream to catch the floating pail after Ted put it in.

Again and again they ran along the road to trade places. By mid-afternoon, both boys were tired, but there was time for one more turn. This time Arlin took the calfy pail an especially long way up the ditch. He waved to Ted that he was about the launch the boat, and Ted waved back. Arlin set the pail in again, and it began bobbing down toward Ted as before. What a long trip it would have this time, they both thought!

Arlin sat down on the ditch bank to watch and rest. At the other end, Ted saw that it would be a while before the pail reached him, so he sat down on the ditch bank too. He looked at the white, fluffy clouds and thought about flying in a hot air balloon. From up there he would be able to see the calfy pail floating down the ditch. Suddenly Ted remembered. "The calfy pail!" he thought, jumping up to see it bobbing past him toward the barn.

Arlin had already seen the disaster from up the road, and he yelled, "The calfy pail! The calfy pail! Ted! Ted! Get the calfy pail!"

Arlin was coming closer, running until his lungs burned and everything looked red to him. Ted was running as fast as he could too, but the pail was still ahead of him. He was gaining on it when it floated into the driveway culvert. He knew he would be near it when it came out the other side in front of the lawn.

Ted slid down near the ditch, holding onto a clump of grass to avoid falling in. He was just level with the pail when it came out, and he grabbed for it. Just then the current pushed the pail to the other side of the ditch, and it floated out of reach. Both boys began running madly to catch up. But it was no use. The calfy pail was swallowed up in the mouth of the scary drain tile that led to the river.

"It's gone! It's gone!" Ted yelled, starting to cry. "We lost the calfy pail!"

Arlin was furious with Ted. Why hadn't he caught the pail? Suddenly Arlin heard himself yelling at Ted. "Ted! Ted! You old spitter! You old brat!" He didn't know where those words came from, especially "spitter." His mind must have made up that awful word just for this emergency.

Arlin wasn't crying yet, but he thought that this terrible accident was probably about the worst thing that had ever happened in the whole world. What would happen to the calfies? What would happen to *him*? He pushed from his mind his father's stern warnings about playing with the calfy pail. He had to think fast.

"The river!" he yelled. "We'll catch it at the river! Run to the river!"

Arlin was off and running down the road before Ted saw through his tears where he was going. Ted choked off his crying and did his best to keep up with his playmate, who was already far ahead.

Arlin knew where the drain tile emptied into the river at the end of the road. The calfy pail would have to come out there. A boy with a long stick might be able to fish it out when it came floating by. He could see that there was just enough room to stand beside the mouth of the tunnel without being swept into the even more dangerous water in the river. With one hand, he held onto a sturdy little tree while he waited with a long stick to catch the runaway calfy pail.

"Did you catch the calfy pail yet?" Ted yelled when he arrived.

"Not yet. I'm waiting for it."

"Can you really catch it with that stick?" Ted asked, wondering if the plan would work.

"I hope so," Arlin said with a sinking feeling. What if the calfy pail didn't come out? What if it was already in the river? What if it came out but went past them again?

The boys waited and waited for the calfy pail to come out. Nothing happened. Arlin had to climb up on the bank and rest his arms a couple of times, always ready to lunge back toward the water to catch the calfy pail if it did come through. Finally it was time to give up. The calfy pail was a goner. The two boys walked wearily and fearfully toward home.

At Arlin's house they parted, and Ted started for his house, eager to leave Arlin to his fate. They both knew not to tell anyone. What they had done was such a bad thing that they didn't want anyone to know. But how would Arlin explain the missing calfy pail? And what would happen to the hungry calfies?

Arlin wondered what would happen when Ma and Pa learned the calfy pail was lost. What would he tell Ma? What would Pa say? What would he do? He tried not to think about the razor strop, that piece of leather his father kept behind the pantry door, the one he used for spankings.

"Are you and Ted all right?" Ma asked as Arlin stepped almost silently into the mud porch and slipped off his boots, placing them next to all the other muddy shoes and boots the family kept there.

"Yup," he said as calmly as possible in response, wondering what was next.

"You lost the calfy pail, din' ya?" she said quietly.

His heart slammed hard against his chest and then seemed to stop. *"She knows! This is it! This is the end!"* he thought. *"The calfy pail really is gone, and Ma knows who lost it and how."*

"How did you know?" Arlin blurted out, nearly crying.

"I seen you and Ted with it down at the ditch, and you scared me half a death, yelling your way to the river. Ain't nobody in Leatherport dint hear about the calfy pail before it hit the river," Ma replied matter-of-factly, still stirring something at the stove.

"If only I hadn't yelled. Why wasn't I quiet? Why did Ted have to cry?" Arlin thought silently, staring at the other side of the kitchen,

"I'll tell your pa how you tried to catch it ennaway," Ma said reassuringly.

What she had just said was his only hope. He <u>did</u> try to catch the calfy pail, even when it was dangerous. He had been brave. Maybe Pa would take pity on him.

That night Arlin was in the corncrib shelling more corn for the chickens when his father came home. Arlin had decided it would be a good time to shell even more corn. Pa went in the house, but Arlin didn't hear any sounds of angry talking. It might be a good sign.

Finally Ma called everyone to supper. The other children were already in when Arlin approached the house. He could hear laughing inside, and he wondered if he would ever be able to laugh again. The laughing stopped when he entered the mud porch. Carefully he kicked off his boots and stepped to the kitchen door. Everyone looked at him.

"I hear you lost the calfy pail," Pa said as he finished washing his hands, sounding very much to Arlin like the Lord when he found the children of Israel sinning. Pa then looked straight into Arlin's eyes. "Well, I guess you'll have to get the calfy a new pail," Pa said. "Got any money?"

Arlin looked at Pa. That's all Pa said about the calfy pail. All Arlin could think was that Pa must be very tired. He watched as Pa hung up the towel and walked slowly to his place at the table and sat down, looking over the steaming food. "Let's eat," he said. Everyone joined him at the table and passed the food. Even Arlin felt like eating.

It was a very good supper that night, and it was better the next night when no more had been said about the calfy pail all day. Arlin gave Ma the money he had been saving for a toy airplane, and Pa bought a new calfy pail at the grain elevator in town. Before long, the three calfies became so big they didn't need the new calfy pail anymore, and Arlin never, ever touched the new calfy pail.

Arlin and Ted made frequent trips to the river to see if the old calfy pail might have come out and caught on a tree or a root or a rock at the end of the tunnel. They looked for many weeks, but it never came out. In summer, when the ditch was dry, they crawled part of the way into the tunnel to see if they could find the calfy pail, but they had no luck. They didn't crawl all the way to the river. That was too dangerous, and there might have been snakes or other animals hiding in there.

Ted and Arlin grew up and moved away, and Arlin told the story to my brothers and sisters and me many years later. When we grew up, we told the story to our children. I took my kids to the river several times to look for the calfy pail, even though by then it had been sixty or seventy years since the pail was lost.

No one ever found the calfy pail, but even now, when I visit Leatherport I still ask people, "Do you think the calfy pail is still stuck in the drain tile?" Those who know the story laugh, and some ask me to tell it again.

Part Five

SAMPLE STORIES FROM *THE CLOCK*

OF THE COVENANT

Sample Stories from *The Clock of the Covenant*

*A*s an impressionable young boy, I misunderstood the minister when he preached about the biblical ark of the covenant. In my childish mind, the old schoolhouse clock in our one-room church building became the "clock of the covenant." In my mind, it was the container in which members of our church had brought the promises of God from Egypt to Elmore, Ohio. This ancient and sacred clock witnessed serious and silly things that happened in our little congregation.

These stories have been written mainly for adult audiences to enjoy, but some may be fun for kids. The following stories appear in The Clock of the Covenant, *a collection of tales from northwestern Ohio (to be released in 2016 or later).*

How the Clock Got Its Name

Religious consciousness awakened abruptly for me one Sunday morning when I was a young boy. I emerged from the formless, larval stage of my religious life while I was standing, facing the back of a one-room church, balancing precariously on the edge of a folding wooden theatre seat.

As I rocked on the seat, attempting to pass time while the adults were preoccupied with activities up front, something drew my attention to the back wall of the church, to a mysterious box on the wall. I already knew it to be a clock, but it was a very special clock, not like the one at home. Under the clock's face, inside a small glass housing, a pendulum swung back and forth. Between outbursts of worshipful preaching and shouting, I could hear the clock ticking its ancient sounds as its pendulum moved in rhythm with the words.

Even then, I sensed authority in that clock and its ceaseless ticking. The pendulum itself bore a golden design that looked to me like a face. As I rocked and stared, it seemed to become the face of one of the Philistine gods I had heard about in Sunday school stories. I imagined it to be one of the wicked gods destroyed in the Israelites' conquest of the Promised Land.

The swinging pendulum may have induced a partial hypnotic trance in me, for I seemed to hear words that settled deep into my consciousness and took on extraordinary significance: "And when Moses came down from Mt. Sinai with the tablets of the Law, he ordered that the tablets be placed in the ark of the covenant to be carried wherever God's people went." In my boyhood imagination, I thought the preacher up front had just said that the promises of God were locked in the "clock of the covenant" to be a reminder forever of God's laws and His love.

The clock *was* mysterious and ancient, something our spiritual forebears must have carried with them out of the desert until they reached Elmore. Indeed, there *was* a door on the face of the clock, perhaps where the promises had been placed. And there it hung, still with God's people, the people in my church in Elmore, Ohio.

I am one of the few still living who saw the clock of this story in its place in the old, one-room church on Clinton Street in Elmore, Ohio. Perhaps my life has been extended to this point so I can tell you what I saw and heard during my growing up years in that little church in a little town as ordinary as the town of Bethlehem.

New Year's Eve

The sacred hush of Christmas Eve 1949 gave way the next morning to the excitement of Christmas Day. My brothers and I opened presents as usual in the early morning and played with our new toys. If we were lucky, snow would be falling sometime soon, and the pond would have enough ice for skating.

The week after Christmas sped by in a dizzying sequence of playing with toys and seeing the neighbor kids and our cousins. We were allowed to stay up every night past our usual bedtimes. After all, it was Christmas break with no school. After the days of playing and holiday eating, we were excited about the next great event: New Year's Eve.

I had heard of New Year's Day, the first day of the new year, and I knew about New Year's Eve, the actual time when one year passed away and a new one was born, but I had never taken part in any celebration of it. We kids had always gone to bed too early. Now that I was ten years old, I understood that years change numbers on New Year's Eve, just like my age changed on my birthday. The day took on special new importance.

I was thrilled when my parents announced that we would go to church at about ten o'clock at night and stay there until midnight. I had never stayed up that long or that late. I began to wonder what it would look like when the New Year came. Would there be a line across the sky just as the New Year arrived so we could tell the difference between the New Year and the old one? Would the new sky have a brighter color? Would the stars be bigger and brighter? One thing I did know. I wanted to be outside, looking up at the sky, at the actual moment of midnight.

My parents explained that our church would have a "Watch Night Service." Everyone would "watch and pray" as the New Year approached and then sing, stand, and kneel before God as it arrived. We often knelt to pray in church, and I felt certain we would kneel at least once during this special service.

The Watch Night Service seemed awesome and holy to me, just the kind of thing that the people in Bible stories might have done. I still thought the people in our church were pretty much the same as the "children of Israel," especially since I thought they had brought the Clock of the Covenant all the way to Elmore, Ohio. But I was worried about all the singing, standing, praying, and preaching we had to get through before the New Year arrived. I wanted to be outside at the moment the New Year began. What if we were late?

The New Year's Eve Watch Night Service began with solemn singing and Scripture reading in the sanctuary followed by a short sermon about commitment and devotion to God. Then the men and boys and the women and girls went to separate rooms in the basement to wash each other's feet like Jesus had washed the disciples' feet before he was crucified.

In those basement rooms, people paired up to wash each other's feet in metal basins of water, mercifully warmed for this purpose.

While washing my feet, one of the older men talked quietly about God's love and the humility of Jesus. The same thing was going on all around our room, and presumably in the room for women and girls. The end of the old year was like the end of a time in our lives, and we were finishing it just as Jesus had ended the time of his earthly ministry.

After foot washing, we returned to the sanctuary and sat quietly. Aunt Lucille played a slow, thoughtful hymn on the organ, and we were instructed to think about the passing of the year, the passing of our lives, and the holy importance of the year ahead.

When everyone was back in the sanctuary, it was time for communion, which we called "The Lord's Supper." Brother Lee, our pastor, reminded everyone of the seriousness of taking communion and of the danger of taking communion unworthily. Then he began to recite the sacred lines about Jesus breaking bread and telling the disciples it represented his body.

After all of the instructions about how to receive the bread and the grape juice, symbolic of Jesus' body and blood, we went row by row to kneel at the altar for communion. As we each ate a piece of bread and drank a tiny cup of juice, we were enacting something Jesus had done near the end of his life on earth. The organ was played softly again, and again we were instructed to think, this time about the shortness of life and our purpose for being here on earth.

I peeked at the sacred clock on the wall. I saw that it was 11:50 p.m., only ten minutes before midnight. Now the swift passing of our lives became more urgent and more important to me. We needed to get the church service finished before midnight so we could actually see the New Year arrive.

I watched and waited for something to happen, but people just sat there, praying silently, while the time on the clock kept moving forward. Finally at about 11:55 p.m., Brother Lee stood and said it would be fitting for us to begin the New Year in prayer. He asked everyone to kneel in the pews so we could "pray in the New Year."

We all knelt to pray inside the church, but my heart sank when I thought that I might not be outside when the New Year swept across the sky. We prayed and prayed, and finally Brother Lee said that the New Year had arrived. We stood, and he gave a closing prayer.

Just as Brother Lee said "Amen," there was a loud boom outside. Unable to wait another second, I ran to the back of the church and out the door to see the sky. Another boom sounded, and I looked to see the line in the sky I had imagined.

The night was clear, and the stars were bright, but I couldn't tell where the New Year began and the old one left off. I had missed the actual midnight moment. I had missed seeing the line across the sky. The New Year had come when we were praying. The booms we had heard were large fireworks shot off a couple of blocks away, not the sound of the New Year crossing the sky.

Other kids came out, and we listened to the noises in the night. Firecrackers were set off a few blocks away, people banged on pan lids, and a bell rang at a church on the other side of town.

Suddenly we heard blam blam! Both barrels of a double-barreled shotgun were fired one after the other only a couple of houses away. "Somebody is shooting a shotgun!" one of the kids yelled. We waited for the gun to be fired again, but for a moment the night was quiet.

Then we heard something we hadn't heard before: ping ping ping followed by a more rapid ping ping ping ping. All along the row of parked cars in front of the church the pinging sounded like a rain shower beginning, only sharper.

"It's the bullets landing!" yelled one of the kids. "The shotgun bullets are landing!"

Just then we heard more shotgun blasts. Blam! Blam! They were coming from the same yard they'd come from before. We waited for the ping ping ping and then the more rapid ping ping ping ping ping to come again.

"Yea! Yea!" we cheered and ran back into the church to tell the others. By the time everyone else was outside, the night was quiet again, so we kids had to tell everyone about the shotgun bullets landing on the cars. Some of the women thought this was a terrible thing, but some of the men said it probably wouldn't hurt anything.

While the grown-ups finished talking, we kids listened for more sounds of the New Year, but all was quiet and still. Soon we were snuggling down in the back seats of our parents' cars, heading home for our first sleep of the New Year.

It had been a good way to end the old year: a church service that included washing feet, having the Lord's Supper, singing, and praying in the New Year. I didn't see the line across the sky when the New Year came, but I heard something even better: powerful blasts from a shotgun and the clatter of pellets landing on cars. Surely it was a good start to the New Year, and 1950 would be a wonderful year of peace and happiness.

GRANDPA WEBERT'S PANTS

Grandpa Webert wasn't my Grandpa. He was the grandpa of my cousin Norman Webert. To me Grandpa Webert seemed ancient. He was ancient because he was very old, and he was ancient because he came from another country. Actually, he came from two foreign countries, Germany and Latvia, and he spoke German.

As a boy of only ten, I thought Grandpa Webert's appearance was very strange and ancient. He had large, rounded shoulders, and he stooped forward when he stood or walked his slow, shuffling walk. He had a big, bushy moustache and large, black eyebrows. His clothes made him look old and foreign too. He wore suspenders and dull-colored, baggy pants. He seldom spoke, partly because of his poor English, partly because he was shy, and partly because he was nearly deaf.

Grandma Webert seemed even older and more foreign than Grandpa Webert. She was probably a few years younger, but still she seemed older. She kept her gray hair tied tightly in a bun, and she wore long, drooping dresses and a shawl that covered her shoulders. She spoke even less than Grandpa Webert. In fact, I don't think I ever heard her speak at all.

Grandpa and Grandma Webert always came to church early, and they always sat in the third pew from the front on the left-hand side. To see them there every Sunday was like a message of truth that the Scriptures were everlasting. Everyone could count on Grandpa and Grandma Webert to be there, even if people mostly couldn't understand them when they talked, which they seldom did.

It was especially solemn and awesome on the times when the minister asked Grandpa Webert to pray in his native German language. Whenever that happened, everyone stood for prayer, and a hush came over the people. Grandpa Webert took a few moments to collect his thoughts. He may have been praying silently in those moments before he began to pray aloud in German. Then he began marching out his prayer in his old, raspy voice. His German words seemed holier than most prayers in English. God understood Grandpa Webert's prayer, and the rest of us knew we had listened in on a special conversation.

Grandpa Webert's prayer began quietly but urgently, seeming to me like a deep conversation with God in a special language that God alone understood. It was the closest thing to a Latin language service most of us in our church ever experienced. Sacredness was clothed in another language. The only thing we did understand of Grandpa Webert's prayer was his "Amen" at the end, the same as English. And it always was followed by a loud "Amen!" from Uncle Fred Webert and other older people as we sat down.

Another glimpse into Grandpa Webert's world came on Christmas Eve. When Uncle Fred was the song leader, he would sing "Silent Night" in German as a special treat for everyone. Others in our church knew some German, not just Grandpa and Grandma Webert.

"Stille nacht, heilege nacht," Uncle Fred sang. Those sitting near the front could see the tears rolling down Grandpa Webert's cheeks. He took out his big blue handkerchief and wiped his eyes and blew his nose. I didn't know German, but I could envision an old German church, deep snow, and a mysterious European forest as Uncle Fred sang "Silent Night."

One summer during Sunday night church, Grandma and Grandpa Webert were in their usual place in the front of the church, and everyone else was farther back. Many rows of empty pews were between the older Webert's and the "young people," as we kids were called, in the back two rows. The service began as usual with an opening song, an opening prayer, another song, and then another. When the singing stopped, the pastor stepped to the pulpit and talked about our blessings and about troubles and illness in the world. He then said, "Let's all stand and go to the Lord in prayer."

People shuffled to their feet. We bowed our heads, and the pastor began to pray. Up front Grandpa Webert placed his huge, calloused hands on the pew in front of him and bowed his head. I guessed he was praying in his German language. The pastor's prayer ended after a few minutes, and he concluded with a very quiet "Amen."

Everyone sat down except Grandpa Webert. He was too deaf to hear the pastor's "Amen," and he was deep in his own silent prayer. Possibly he had fallen asleep while standing. The pastor looked at Grandpa Webert still standing there. He didn't know what to do except go on with the service, so he began reading a passage from the Bible.

None of us kids were paying attention to the pastor. We were only looking at Grandpa Webert, still standing and praying, stooped over the pew in front of him. We saw his huge shoulders, his suspenders, and his baggy pants. To the unruly "young people" at the back of the church, he looked odd, and his behavior was so strange that we nudged each other and began to laugh, some of us pretty loudly.

Grandma Webert had better hearing than Grandpa Webert, so the disturbance at the back of the church caught her attention. She looked back and saw us laughing, and she scowled at us. To our complete surprise, she then reached up and grabbed Grandpa Webert by the seat of his pants, attempting to make him sit down.

Grandpa Webert didn't seem to notice, or maybe he just chose to ignore her, so she pulled again, harder. This time when she pulled, Grandpa Webert's suspenders stretched, and his pants sagged dangerously. Everyone gasped! Grandma Webert had nearly pulled down Grandpa Webert's pants! When Grandma Webert tugged again, Grandpa Webert finally looked at her and sat down.

The uproar in the young people's pews subsided a little. All of us laughed and poked each other and whispered our own accounts of what had just happened. It was one of the funniest things we had ever seen in church. It must have been the funniest thing Grandma and Grandpa Webert had ever done.

Grandpa Webert may never have known what happened. He couldn't have heard our laughter. But Grandma Webert did hear the laughing and knew what happened. She was probably very ashamed. How could she have done such a lewd thing, pulling at Grandpa Webert's pants until they nearly came down? It even happened in church! But she hadn't meant to do such a terrible thing. God would forgive her, she probably reasoned later that week. But would God forgive those unruly young people who had laughed so hard? Maybe he would, provided they repented.

Grandma Webert must have wondered to herself what Grandpa Webert knew or thought about the incident. As far as I know, she never told him what had happened. The story of Grandpa Webert's pants went into a deep closet of forgetfulness at the Webert's farmhouse, and

Grandma and Grandpa Webert went safely their home in heaven in the 1950s, taking this secret story with them.

Since Grandma Webert never told Grandpa Webert about his pants, I hope I can trust you to never, ever tell if you see Grandpa Webert in heaven someday.

Questions for Conversations

*T*he questions that follow are provided to encourage imagination and elaboration.

Why the House Was Called Brown

  a. Have you ever experienced living for a short period of time without electricity and running water? What was it like?
  b. Draw a picture of the outside of your house.
  c. How is your house different from the Brown House?

Seeing the World from the Windmill

  a. Have you ever seen a farm windmill? What did it look like?
  b. What is the highest place you have climbed?
  c. If you could go any place in the world, where would you go?
  d. Have you ever seen a waterwheel? How is it alike or different from a windmill?

e. Have you ever helped somebody in trouble the way Merl helped in the story?

The Beacon Light

a. Which of the following ways to travel have you experienced so far: airplane, bus, train, boat, and subway? What are some ways you would like to travel?

b. How are parents sometimes like a beacon light?
Suggested reading: *The Little Red Lighthouse* by Hildegard H. Swift, *Keep the Lights Burning, Abby* by Peter Roop.

Train Whistle Blowing

a. Where have you heard a train whistle blowing?

b. What do trains carry today?

c. Where would you like to go on a train?

d. Why does a train need a whistle or horn?

e. Did you ever have a train set? What did you imagine when you played with it?

Graytown Park

a. What did you do that was the most fun you have had in a park? Where was it?

b. What kind of rides did that park have? Which was your favorite?

c. What is the most dangerous thing you have done in a park?

d. How can you compare the centrifugal force of the merry-go-round with the movement of the planets?

e. Is it good or bad to take risks at a playground? What could happen?

Our Own Merry-Go-Round

a. What is the most fun thing to do in your yard?

b. What's the most fun thing you do at home with your family now?

c. When you grow up, what kind of fun things will you have in your yard for your kids?

d. If you could design a new piece of playground equipment, what would it be like?

e. What kind of toys have you created and played with that were made from objects around your house such as boxes, towels, tubes, rubber bands?

Fire Made from Dirt

a. Besides putting dirt on a fire, what else can be done to put out fires?

b. If there is a fire at your house, what should you do?

c. What wrong idea did you have when you were little like the boy in this story who thought he could start a fire by digging dirt?

d. Where and how do firefighters use trenches to stop fires?

Going Swimming

a. Where did you wade in water before you were old enough to go swimming?

b. What was the silliest, littlest place that you used to think was a swimming pool?

c. Where would you like to swim now?

d. Where have you gone swimming, including pools, ponds, rivers, creeks, lakes, and oceans?

e. What are some ways that you cool off in your own backyard on a hot summer day?

f. How did your feelings about being in deep water change as you became older and possibly better at swimming?

Hiding in the Smokehouse

a. Have your parents or grandparents ever seen a smokehouse and told you what it was like?

b. What is the dirtiest place where you ever hid?

c. What outdoor games do you like to play with your family and friends?

d. Which of the five senses did you feel most strongly in this story?

e. Do you like to be scared at the movies, on carnival rides, playing games, or any other place?

Walking on the Water

a. How could you play "Walking on the Water" in your yard?

b. Where have you seen a farm field that was plowed?

c. What story could you and friends act out at your house? What do you think about playing "Jesus Feeding the 5,000" or "David and Goliath" with your friends?

d. Have you ever had courage to try something that you thought was too hard?

Pearl Harbor Day

a. How would you describe what a war is, and what are some of the things that can cause a war?

b. What are the names of some of the wars you have heard of?

c. Have any of your relatives ever been in a war?

d. Why do you think the children at the Brown House were not allowed to play war?

e. What details do you know about World War II? What countries were involved?

"Hear Dem Bells"

a. Do church bells ring near you on Sundays?

b. What do church bells make you think of?

c. How is the place where you live safer than some of the places where other kids live now?

d. What are some ways you might help children who are hungry, homeless, sick, or needing friends near where you live or in some distant part of the world?

Brown Sugar and Raisins

a. What is your favorite special treat?

b. Can you describe a time when you felt lonely when your parents were away from home?

c. If you were sad about your parents going away for an evening or longer, what made you feel better?

d. Do you think it was wrong or right for the boy's mother to leave him and his brothers with a babysitter?

Escaping the Babysitter

   a. What reasons do parents have for hiring babysitters?

   b. If you are ever a babysitter, what will you do to be nice to the kids?

Going to See the Hole

   a. Have you ever seen a hole in the ground before a house or school was built or after a building was torn down? Where was it?

   b. If you have ever seen a building being torn down, what did it look like and sound like?

   c. Where in your neighborhood is a place you can go only when you are with older kids or grown-ups?

   d. Why do you think the house that used to be above "the hole" was torn down?

   e. When, where, and why have you dug a hole?

   f. What different reasons might people have to dig a hole?

   g. Why do some animals dig holes?
Suggested reading: *Mike Mulligan and His Steam Shovel* by Virginia Lee Burton.

Scaring the Brown House Bear

   a. What do you think about the author's statement that a bear got a ladder and climbed up to look in the window?

   b. Have you ever thought you saw an animal when you w ere sleeping at night?

   c. What would you do to scare off a bear at your house?

   d. What do you think the Brown House bear actually was?

   e. Suggested reading: *Goldilocks and the Three Bears*. Related question: How is this story like or different from the story of Goldilocks and the three bears?

Stolen Fudge

a. Have you seen anyone eat more than his or her share of a special treat? When did you ever eat more than your share?

b. If you were impolite to an adult today, what would your mother do?

c. What was the Garden of Eden? What happened to the people there after they ate what they were not supposed to eat?

d. When have you had a hard time having self-control about eating or drinking something yummy?

Leaky Lucky

a. What pretend playmates did you or other kids have when you were younger?

b. Why do some kids have pretend playmates?

c. What favorite stuffed animal or special blanket did you or do you still sleep with? How is it like or different from having a pretend friend?

d. How is a pretend friend better than a real friend?

e. How is a real friend better than a pretend friend?
Suggested reading: *Ira Sleeps Over* by Bernard Waber.

Tragedy Roars By

a. What dangerous thing *almost* happened to someone in your family but *didn't* happen?

b. When have you seen grownups cry because they were happy? What made them so happy they cried?

c. What are your mother's rules about where you can play outside?

d. How could the workers and Mama understand each other when they did not speak the same language?

Questions for Conversations

Riding the Tomato Planter

   a. When have you seen farm workers planting something in a large field?

   b. What crops have you seen when traveling through farm areas?

   c. What grown-up things did you like to pretend to do when you were younger?

   d. Do you think "play" can ever be a part of "work"? Can real work be fun?

   e. Have you planted seeds and taken care of them as they were growing or bought a tomato plant and planted it outside?

The Pear

   a. Why did the boys think they would be able to eat "the pair?"

   b. What other words sound alike but have very different meanings?

   c. Did you ever have a surprise you didn't want? What happened?

   d. Would you like to draw some pictures of words that are homonyms, which means they sound the same but have different meanings?

   e. Can you think of a silly sentence with homonyms in it like this one: The bear was bare? Another: The pair of boys ate the pear.

Leaving the Brown House

   a. Has your family always lived in the house where you live now?

   b. If you have lived in a different house than where you live right now, what was that house like?

   c. If you ever have to move to a different house, what will you make sure to take with you?

d. Have your parents and grandparents told you things about you when you were much younger? What was the most interesting thing they told you about yourself?

e. What would you miss if you had to move from your house?

f. What would you look forward to if you were to move to a new house?

g. What are some things that you think you will tell your own children someday about your childhood? Do you think you could have your own "Brown House" stories to tell?

Background Information

For some stories, historical and geographical background information can add to the understanding of time and place. The information that follows is grouped according to story title and may be interesting when reading a particular story.

If you were to visit Graytown, Ohio, and drive past the Brown House today, it wouldn't seem like a place of adventure and fun. The land would look flat and ordinary. If you had driven past the Brown House in the 1940s, you would not have seen most of these stories as they happened. The stories in this book show that there is "more than meets the eye" in ordinary places. It can take many years for the significance of stories to be recognized even by those who are living them, and it may take even more years for anyone to write the stories down.

The flat farm country along Graytown Road in Northern Ohio conceals things hidden underground and things buried in the past. Under the ground is amazingly rich soil and dense clay. Beneath the soil and clay is a layer of limestone. These natural resources are used for farming, industry, and building material. Below them are scattered deposits of natural gas. If you were to tunnel far below the limestone and gas, you would approach the center of the Earth, where it's always hot. That adventure, of course, goes beyond the scope of *The Brown House Stories*.

An important fact you might not know if you were walking or riding your bike along the Graytown Road is that it is near Lake Erie and not far from Canada. Lake Erie is one of the gifts of the last glacier that covered parts of Ohio. The soil, clay, and limestone deposits underground are also gifts of the glacier. That glacier finally melted about 10,000 years ago. For more about Ohio's earliest natural history, you may wish to visit http://www.ohiohistorycentral.org/w/Bedrock_Geology_of_Ohio.

Less than two hundred years ago the area around the Brown House was within what early settlers named the Black Swamp. Only isolated stands of uncut forest from that time period now remain in the middle of farmland in the area, but the Black Swamp had a nearly mythical hold on our minds as my brothers and I grew up where it once was. Bears, bobcats, and wild boars once inhabited the Black Swamp. Today there are only smaller animals such as raccoons, opossums, muskrats, weasels, fox, turtles, snakes, and many kinds of birds. To learn more about the Black Swamp, you may wish to visit http://en.wikipedia.org/wiki/Great_Black_Swamp and http://www.hicksville-ohio.com/History/blackswamp.htm.

Seeing the World from the Windmill
The windmill at the Brown House was very different from the enormous, airplane-like machines you see on modern wind farms. Those modern windmills are called wind turbines, and most are over 300 feet tall. They capture wind energy and turn it into electrical power. Farm windmills like those at the Brown House, in contrast, were usually about 20 feet tall and had four wooden or metal legs. Their function was to pump water, and in some places they are still used.

Farm windmills are less common today because gasoline engines and electric motors can more reliably pump water. In some places in the United States windmills still exist, mainly out West. Some still depend on wind power, while others are operated by solar-powered electric pumps.

The pumps maintain the water level in water tanks where cattle can get drinks in open country. You may see these tanks and occasional windmills along the roadsides as you travel from city to city in farm country. For more information on windmills, you may visit http://plainshumanities.unl.edu/encyclopedia/doc/egp.ii.062.

This and other stories may make you wonder how children growing up in the time of these stories survived to adulthood given the amount of playtime they experienced without watchful adult supervision. In another collection of stories called *Leatherport Tales*, you will find that most kids in the 1940s and 1950s had hours of unsupervised play every day during summer vacations. This "free-range parenting" is in sharp contrast to the more modern phenomenon of overprotective parents, sometimes called "helicopter parents" for their hovering behavior.

Due to fears for children's safety, neighbors, police, and child protective services have joined forces to prevent children from having the independence many children enjoyed decades ago. A *Time* magazine article in 2015 told the story of a couple reported to police for allowing their children (ages 10 and 6) to play in a local park and walk two blocks to their home without adult supervision. For more information on changing parenting styles, see the following:

http://time.com/3841466/free-range-parenting-2-0/
http://www.freerangekids.com/
http://thefederalist.com/2015/04/28/the-hyped-dangers-of-free-range-parenting/

The Beacon Light
The beacon light near the Brown House probably was about 50 feet tall, a standard height in those times. Beacon lights were first used along

certain air mail routes, starting in 1922, to guide planes to help them deliver mail and packages in the fastest way. Planes that flew only in daylight delivered mail only a little faster than high-speed trains. Air mail was only an expensive novelty before beacon lights were installed for night flights. Daylight flights depended on maps, visible landmarks, and sometimes giant arrows placed in fields and on mountains to aid pilots.

By 1926, there were 14,500 miles of lighted airways in the United States, and air mail became practical. Daring pilots trusted their lives at night to their own skills and the beacon lights. Navigation beacon lights were phased out after World War II when radar became common. For more information on early aircraft navigation, you may wish to visit http://www.navfltsm.addr.com/howitbegan.htm.

Train Whistle Blowing

Railroad construction in Ohio was slow before 1840 but expanded dramatically after the Civil War (1861–1865). The New York Central railroad line through Graytown remains heavily traveled by freight trains and the occasional Amtrak passenger train. Although many rail lines have been abandoned in all parts of the country, railroads are still important for carrying heavy bulk materials such as coal, oil, iron ore, farm products, stone, cars, and trucks.

Our Own Merry-Go-Round

In addition to the creation described in this story, my dad also attached a swing very high in a tree so my siblings and I could fly out over the pond and drop in to swim far from shore. The zip line was his most popular ride. At age 90, he persuaded some of his young grandchildren to give him a ride on it. The inattentive adults were shocked, but they laughed to see the 90-year old man flying down the zip line, grinning with is feet outstretched, just like hundreds of kids before him.

Walking on the Water

The imagination of my brothers and me was fueled by the story of Jesus walking on the water, as told in Matthew 14:22–34; Mark 6:45–53; and John 6:15–21.

Pearl Harbor Day

Perhaps the majority of Americans learned about the Japanese attack on Pearl Harbor on December 7, 1941, on the radio. My parents didn't have electricity or a radio, so my mother heard of it through the landlord. Undoubtedly millions of others learned of the attack in this way, from another person. For more information on that day, you may wish to visit this website designed for young students: http://www.ducksters.com/history/world_war_ii/pearl_harbor_attack.php.

"Hear Dem Bells"

My family's branch of the Kardatzke name is traced to the town of Stolp in Prussia, now known as Slupsk in current Poland. It is about 40 miles west of Gdansk, Poland. Stolp was less severely damaged than many other German cities in World War II, but the Soviet Army burned the entire central city in 1945.

Escaping the Babysitter

The term babysitter seems to have originated in 1937. Until then, mothers and older siblings "minded the children." World War II gave rise to modern babysitting because so many women entered the workforce and also family relationships were disrupted by wartime travel. For more on the rise and fall of babysitting, you may wish to visit http://www.faqs.org/childhood/Ar-Bo/Baby-Sitters.html.

Going to See the Hole

The book mentioned at the end of the story was one of the *Dick and Jane* school readers that were widely used from 1930 until the 1960s. *Dick and Jane* books developed word recognition through the "look and say" method. Other reading instruction materials focused on phonics and the logic of language. I have never been a fast or efficient reader, but *Dick and Jane* probably shouldn't be blamed; it was probably due to a character flaw. For more information, you may search the Internet using the search term "Dick and Jane Books" and examine a few of the first twelve million hits.

Scaring the Brown House Bear

Bears were common in Ohio before the state was settled, but they were driven from the state by about 1870. They now are returning to places in eastern Ohio and flourish in the imaginations of a few Ohio children. For more information on bears in Ohio, you may wish to visit http://www.ohiohistorycentral.org/w/Black_Bear.

Leaky Lucky

My older brother, Merl, now denies that Leaky Lucky moved with us to the Brown House. I won't let his memory of the facts stand in the way of a good story. Merl was only four years old when we moved to the Brown House. If he had already invented Leaky Lucky by then, he must have had a precocious imagination.

I didn't read the *Psychology Today* article that I reference here until after I wrote this story. I'm gratified to find that my story fits reality quite well. You may wish to read about children's imaginary friends by visiting https://www.psychologytoday.com/blog/growing-friendships/201301/imaginary-friends.

Tragedy Roars By

Throughout my childhood, I had contact with Hispanic farm workers, men, women, and children that we simply called Mexicans. Some may have come from Mexico under the Braceros Program of guest workers during World War II, but most in fact were from Texas. Although they lived in humble cabins in Ohio during the summer, some of those workers had fine brick homes in Texas.

Mechanization of farming and collective bargaining have reduced the importance of this kind of farm labor. To learn more about migrant and seasonal workers, you may wish to read the "Short History" section of this website: http://www.jsri.msu.edu/upload/research-reports/rr01.pdf.

Riding the Tomato Planter

Ohio is the third largest tomato growing state in the United States, after California and Indiana. A modern tomato planting machine can be seen in this YouTube video: https://www.youtube.com/watch?v=CnQfaxmFHx4.

About the Author

Nyle Kardatzke lives in Indianapolis, Indiana. He spent his boyhood in farm country east of Toledo, Ohio, from 1939 to 1957. After graduating from Elmore High School, he left Ohio to attend Anderson University in Anderson, Indiana.

After college graduation in 1962, Nyle taught math and science to Eritrean students as a member of the first Peace Corps group in what was then part of Ethiopia. Intrigued by the struggles of less developed countries, he returned home and earned a doctorate in economics at the University of California, Los Angeles (UCLA). He taught economics at Marquette University in Milwaukee for a few years but spent the bulk of his professional career as Headmaster in private schools in Wisconsin, Kansas, and Indiana.

In 2014 Nyle published *Widow-man: A Widower's Story and Journaling Book* for widowed men like himself. His wife, Darlene, died in 2010. Nyle intends to publish two more collections of stories in the near future. He has three adult children and nine grandchildren who enjoy hearing him tell and retell the stories from his childhood years in Ohio.

CPSIA information can be obtained
at www.ICGtesting.com
Printed in the USA
LVOW04s1711291116

514964LV00024B/583/P